An amusing perspective on the world of
international business

@Global Work collection – Part I

Original Text by Angeline Vagabulle

Illustrations by Renard

English Translation by Andrew Baggaley

To stay up to date with the what's happening #GlobalWorkCollection, you can find us on Facebook here:

https://www.facebook.com/GlobalWorkCollection/

You can also find Angeline Vagabulle on FaceZinZin, LinkGlouGlou, InstaBlurk and Twitbird as well as the author's website:

http://angelinevagabulle.wixsite.com/angelinevagabulle

Thalia NeoMedia / DG Editions Les Funambulles

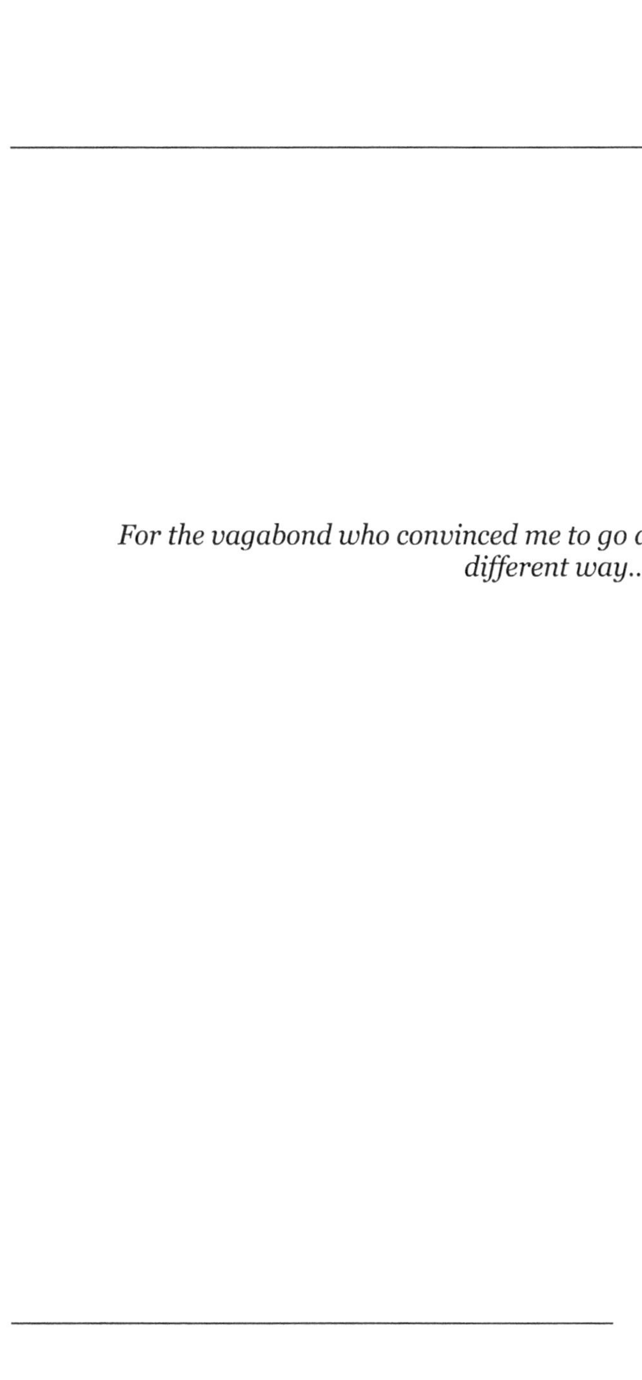

For the vagabond who convinced me to go a different way...

Foreword

Because one day, there was a look. From behind a horrible mixed salad in a no-less horrible brasserie, in an anonymous business district surrounded by skyscrapers, filled with thousands of people distinguishable only by their brand of suit.

Because one day, an exchange of glances can be all it takes for you to see the things around you differently.

Because one day, I decided it was better to simply laugh about it all.

All of the situations described in this work have been inspired by real events, the absurdity of which I felt deserved to be revealed to the wider world.

Companies are Big Theatre

►□◄

Skyscrapers, offices, computers, elevators, meeting rooms, ugly carpets and everything else besides: all of them are just the setting. Because working in an international company is like performing in a theatre. As soon as I understood this fact, I felt a thousand times better about going to work every day. When I walk through the revolving doors into the Big Skyscraper, the red curtain is raised and it's time for me to get into character.

* Rule number one: leave your emotions at the door. You must develop an ability to feign interest in all manner of things that, frankly, are not worth your time.

* Rule number two: wear the right color costume (black, or gray for holidays).

* Rule number three: learn how to not be yourself and instead be the person they expect you to be. This is quite possibly the key to professional success.

When you leave in the evening, you may become yourself again. But what if, hidden behind the gray suits and pink ties, there were people who thought just like you?

Daily Report

10th time wearing the colorful coat.

Saw 352 colleagues in gray suits and 234 in black.

One tea, two coffees.

Skyscrapers

Men created companies. These companies grew larger and became "multinational". In order to house these massive entities, men erected giant towers, symbols of their power.

Old skyscrapers (i.e. ones that were built over ten years ago) are black. Like, really black. Being dark gives them an air of seriousness. I don't need to tell you that when you arrive at work on a cold, gray winter's morning, you really don't feel like entering one of these terrifying towers of doom.

Recently, however, these dark towers have gotten a little lighter in appearance. Now they're gray. Like, really gray. Or sometimes they're just made of glass. Like ships out to conquer new lands, stern against the wind, topsail pointing towards the sky.

Personally, I'm not a fan of feeling like I'm suspended 150m in the air, because that's exactly what being in a skyscraper on the 36th floor means.

Another thing about these enormous towers is that they aren't always square, if we're looking from above. The quest for architects to come up with wacky new shapes for their projects seems to know no limits. I once worked in a building whose shape I never fully managed to comprehend, even after having been around it many times looking for my destination. On the plus side, these escapades did allow me to meet many new people. Another building I worked in was shaped like a triangle. Well, kind of a triangle. Only on certain floors. To have just been one consistent triangle shape would have been far too easy in this crazy world of international business.

Within these skyscrapers, one will find little cubicles that are generously referred to as 'offices'. Obviously, the big bosses' offices are at the top of the tower. Up there, the carpet is thick, and it makes a 'shui-shui' sound as you walk. Go down to the bottom of the building and there you will find the less fortunate souls. The people that work on these floors are the life and blood of the company, whose energy and hard work make sure everything runs smoothly. It's a wonder that the strength of their efforts doesn't make these rocket ships take off sometimes. One has to work very hard indeed to launch a triangle into space, however. Here is where you find the folk that ensure the elevators go up and down, the mail is distributed, the tea and coffee is always hot, as well as all of those other things that keep the fluctuating moods of the workforce in check. They also help maintain the apparatus that recycles the already-recycled air, which is then pumped through pipes directly into your cubicle so you don't suffocate, at least in a literal sense.

Skyscrapers tend to have a center and expand outwards in layers, like an onion. Perhaps it's because like this they are more resistant to attacks from the outside. And of course, it's all about who has the biggest, shiniest... you get the idea. It's a guy thing.

In Paris, where I'm from, the business district is called "La Défense." Most major international organizations with a presence in France have their offices located here. Sat among all of the skyscrapers there is La Grande Arche, a modern update of the world-famous Arc de Triomphe. One only has to look at this new arch, and what surrounds it, to understand what I mean when I say, "it's a guy thing." Big, powerful towers, all crowded around a big arch. I mean, really?

The Uniform

►□◄

You might wonder why I mentioned my colorful coat a little earlier. Well, it's because I'm quite simply fed up with what is considered the mandatory uniform for major international corporations. The suits in gray or black; the blue shirts and pink ties. Yuck! But I'm lucky, I suppose. At least I'm a girl. That being said, if I never saw another white shirt and black cardigan again, it would still be too soon.

So, I started wearing a baseball cap. Then it was the big purple coat. Then a red one. That one was a real winner: you could see me coming from miles away. A little red speck in this monochrome world (the coats, the suits, the skyscrapers, the disjointed paving stones of La Défense, the winter sky, my life, our privileged lives that we're never happy with). When I saw this coat in the window of the store, I decided I was going to crank things up a notch. I immediately saw the potential it had to wake up even the most slumbering of souls. It had all the colors of the rainbow, with funny little sleeves, and all of the joys of life seemed to be stitched upon it.

And guess what? It worked! The last comment I received happened in one of the gray elevators (gray inside and out). A Big Cheese from another international corporation stared at me, eyes wide open, as I entered. His pupils dilated. "Wow! That's a nice coat! Nice to see!" he said. Then, as he left the elevator, he thanked me for this little "moment of happiness." When I saw the light that was in his eyes,

I knew I had done the right thing, buying this coat. It was time to start approaching work fashion a little differently.

The moral of the story: smile, people! You're being watched!

The Acronyms

▶□◀

Acronyms are formed from the initials of other words, making a new word altogether. For example, SCUBA. That's an acronym. It comes from "Self-Contained Underwater Breathing Apparatus."

When SCUBA was invented, acronyms weren't so ubiquitous. It's only with the onslaught of globalization that they've really become so popular. Now, however, they're everywhere, and it seems that no one even bothers to make sure they're pronounceable anymore.

Why do international corporations love them so much anyway? Well, it's because they help us to communicate faster. Because saying, for example, "Human Resources Management Information System" takes too long. Way too long. At least three seconds in fact, and the risk of stuttering as you do so due to all of those pesky long words is deemed to be too high.

So Human Resources Management Information System becomes HRMIS (pronounced "aitch ar em I ess").

So now, whenever something new is introduced within an international corporation, an acronym must be invented to identify it. Whether it's a project, a database, a new process, a department, or anything else. First of all, the name must make logical sense: Department for Uniting Markets and Business, for example. But not so fast: now you have to make sure it can be 'acronymized', and saying that you are the new Head of DUMB doesn't really make you sound too good.

Back to the drawing board.

Head of Building Operations, Markets and Business, that's much better. It's the BOMB, even. No need to go any further, everyone understands that what you do is wonderful. It sounds much better to say that you are now running BOMB. And when you meet people in the corridors or the elevator, you can tell

them with pride. It's surely better than DUMB, in any case.

►□◄

Daily Report

Three times had my hands in the damp, dusty insides of the photocopier.

Twice switched off the light in the restroom.

Sixty-eight emails sent (I sent a lot of invites) and six received (3 of which were spam and two were personal).

One conference call, one call where the line was "busy."

Elevator Operator

▶□◀

So we've already established that large global corporations love to work in Big Skyscrapers. To get around these enormous towers, one is obliged to take an elevator. And when you try to do this during rush hour, you'll inevitably encounter the "Elevator Operator". Don't be fooled, though: this is not the old sense of an elevator operator: a young host or hostess with a nice little uniform who welcomes you, helps you find where you're going, asks how your day is going and tells you which floor you're about to arrive at and what happens there (Whatchamacallit service, Department of Thingamajig, etc.). Nope. Not that. At all.

The new type of elevator operators, known more precisely as "Destination Dispatch" systems, use algorithms to optimize the amount of time that each passenger spends inside the elevator. That means that there's a computer somewhere that calculates the best way to get all of the passengers to all of the floors required in the shortest possible amount of time. The people who are waiting for an elevator are therefore separated into groups at the bottom (of the tower) according to which floor they are going to and to which group of floors their floor belongs. Got it? It's faster that way, apparently.

When the system was first introduced, it did not go down well at all. Figuratively speaking, that is. Because now, instead of waiting inside the elevator as it slowly crept up the floors serving each one in turn, now you had to wait on the ground floor. And when you're waiting on the ground floor, it seems to take much longer than when you're actually, you know, going up. It's psychological. When you're at the bottom, you're not doing anything. But when you're in the elevator, you're... well, you're going up.

It also needs to be said that this system doesn't encourage interaction between colleagues. Imagine that you're at the bottom and you meet someone that you want to talk to. If he or she doesn't happen to work on a floor that's in the same group of floors as yours, you're obliged to separate and say your goodbyes without finishing your conversation. It's a sad way to begin your day. So let's say it how it is: these so-called "elevator operators" are absolutely segregationist.

Fortunately, the trip back down gives us a bit of time for idle chit-chat because the system doesn't work in both directions. At least, it doesn't for now.

Daily Report

Seen on the subway platform: two people sat next to each other, hunched over their phones, both sending messages. I felt like saying to them: "lift up your head, look at each other and talk."

Height of the paper stack accumulating on my desk (sealed and loose): 6 cm (and rising).

Zero messages sent from my phone.

Two coffees, one tea.

Bases

►□◄

In large corporations, there are bases in every direction you look. There's a base for everything, for all kinds of subjects, serving all manners of different functions.

There was a time that a "base" might have meant someplace that you'd go for a little respite; to recharge the batteries. A place where you could relax, gather your thoughts and maybe grab a little bite to eat, before getting back to the realities of work. A nice, useful place. No such luck; in global corporations, that is not what a base is, at all.

Here are a few examples of what a "base" might, in fact, be:

- a database full of information that no one uses.

- a document base that is always empty.

- a database that contains information about other databases.

- a database portal that gives access to other, different databases.

- a "workflow" database, which allows you to automate management processes (and there are many).

- a document base which still contains files from 1998.

- a password database.

- a base where you may request the creation of a new database (oh yes, it exists!)

- a database where incident reports concerning other databases are stored.

- a database of addresses.

- a database of lists (names, email addresses, passwords).

- the base where your emails are received.

- the base where your emails are archived.

- a base containing technical documents.

- the database containing the name of everyone that works for the company.

- a base containing confidential documents.

- a base for reserving a meal tray.

- a base for reserving a parking spot.

- a postal service base.

- a base where you book travel tickets.

- an authorization base where you may request permission to begin a project.

- a base where you request expenses reimbursement.

- a base where you may request the name for a new project.

- a vacation request base.

- a printer base.

As you can see, there a many types of "base" in this type of company. And that means a lot of work for a lot of people:

- there are those who come up with the idea for a new database; usually an assistant manager of some sort from the floor above. They believe that they're making people's lives easier with their creation. Their databases are rarely used at all, and when they are, it's often not for the intended purpose.

- then there are those who either accept or reject the request for a new database (via the base to request the creation of a new database).

- there are those who develop the databases.

- there are those who control the settings for the new database.

- there are the administrators for the new database.

- there are the people who grant group access to the databases.

- there are people who administrate the groups with access to the databases.

- there are people who input data into the database.

- there are people who must maintain the database.

- there is the server upon which the database is stored.

- there are people who must maintain the server upon which the database is stored.

- there are the people who look after the lines of communication between the server and your computer, so that you may access the database.

- there are people who manage the interfaces between the various databases (who was the bright spark that decided to link all of them together?!)

Occasionally, someone, somewhere might use one of them. Whoever they are, they have long been discouraged from doing so. No one really knows if they even still exist. Fortunately for everyone, though, there is the database community base where everyone can go and discuss all things "base", if only to wind down a little.

▶ □ ◀

Daily Report

Spotted this morning at the entry barriers to the Big Skyscraper: a gentleman trying desperately to find his access badge, lost somewhere in his briefcase.

Company of Idiots

In Large Multinational Corporations, about 95% of the employees are management types that have graduated from some of the finest business schools and universities around the world. You would think, therefore, that we're talking about the crème de la crème in terms of raw intellect.

In Large Multinational Corporations, you have what is known as an "Intranet", a tool which is used to explain to these aforementioned super-intelligent people how things need to be done.

In the example below, we can see the explanation for how to order new business cards:

What to do	What not to do
Surname, First name	FIRST NAME, SURNAME; First name, NAME; first name, Surname; first name, surname
Provide your mobile phone number	Don't provide your mobile phone number
Fill in all required fields before submitting form	Forget to fill in all fields and send the form anyway

What to do	What not to do
Do not include the "o" at the beginning of your phone number	Include the "o" at the beginning of your phone number
Don't order the international version unless you are a Department Head	Order the international version if you are not a Department Head
Order 100 business cards at a time	Try to order more

Surely an "Idiots Guide" such as this one has only been placed on the intranet to entertain the employees of the Large Multinational Corporation.

It doesn't stop there, though. Large Multinational Corporations also love to bombard their idiots with nonsense by email. This genuine email was sent by a Chief Financial Officer:

****

Subject: IN ORDER TO CORRECTLY CLOSE A PROJECT, YOU MUST...

* A correctly closed project means:

- opening a new project for the next financial year (when necessary).

- a final budget calculation.

- the saving of this budget, which will retroactively update all records of sales by other business entities.

- an account of the stock corresponding to the last budget calculation.

- the actual closing of the project.

* A very good project closure deletes the manually saved budget by pressing "right off revised balanced", communally known as the "magic button" which calculates and organizes the account automatically.

* A bad project closing does not perform the first two steps, and begins directly with the definitive saving of the final budget, which does not include the updated records of sales (leaving the difference on your project).

* A very bad closure means not having closed anything by the end of the fiscal year.

Please note: if you have saved hours worked or expenses for the previous fiscal year, you may ask your CGM, who knows the procedure, to transfer them to the new number. Only then will the closure come into effect.

****

Personally, I find it extremely interesting to know that in order to correctly close a project, one must indeed have actually closed the project. Fascinating.

Perhaps, in fact, the sender was deliberately trying to be funny.

►□◄

Daily Report

Snacked on three pieces of candy and one chocolate bar to fight the boredom, plus two coffees and one tea.The carpet on the floor of the Big Bosses goes "shui shui" when you walk on it. How has it not worn out already?

Business survival

▶□◀

I've been met by a strange feeling as I came into work on two separate occasions recently. It's a kind of mix between the realization of the true meaning of eternity and my own morbidity. All of this is thanks to global business.

A few months previously to this, a person within my work circle had died. Despite this, his profile on a well-known professional social media platform is still active. Am I still able to conduct business with this person, who now roams in heaven? What if one of my other business contacts asks me to set up a connection with him? What should I say? "Sorry, Bill is no longer of this world; maybe you can get in touch with him when you too have gone to the Big Place in the Sky?"

A few weeks before that, someone else in the company died. That didn't prevent me from sending him an e-mail two days later, though. Is it ok for me to still ask him questions and let him know all about the thrilling goings-on in my life as a businesswoman in a multinational corporation, even though he's kicking around in the heavenly kingdom? If so, would it be alright to ask him to deal with those files that I really don't feel like doing right now?

The feeling of eternity: we now survive past our own death thanks to social networks, thanks to the web in which we shall always to some extent be entangled, thanks to the virtual mails which endure in reality, while we return to a virtual reality.

The feeling of morbidity: the admins who manage things when someone passes from one realm to another must now include in their procedure:

- closing Facezinzin and Linkglouglou accounts,

- ensuring the email account is made inactive (which requires a password),

- setting up an "out of office" that lasts forever:

I am out of office for all of eternity and I won't be coming back. I leave you all of this mess and I'm glad I no longer have to deal with any of it. I am now floating around the heavens, and I don't send you my best wishes. You may contact any of the morons who keep this s***-show of a company going in my absence: maybe you finally be able to give them something to do (yeah, right).

Daily Report

Asked them to install a switch for the toilets that would make it possible to turn off all the lights simultaneously. It would help people like me to save an enormous amount of time because I wouldn't have to go around individually switching each one off in turn.

A Poetic Moment in the Food Court

They're all on the ground, the little love notes from the food court.

They're curled up slightly, rolling in on themselves.

They fly away.

Carried on a current of air – there's no wind to keep them up – so they gently fall to the ground.

They've gone to lay down on the tiles.

And with each pair of feet that passes them, they are launched into a backward somersault, a front twist, a double lateral spin, carried by the gust of air created by the shoes.

What are these little pieces of paper?

They are the checks; each one having escaped from the tray upon which they were so carefully placed, one after the other.

But there's nothing that can stop them.

They should have been trapped underneath a glass (but no, not possible – you get your glass after you've paid), or even under the plate (but not the knife and fork, because like your glass, you get them after you've paid).

And so with nothing to hold them back, they are free to fly through the air.

And until the broom comes to sweep them away, they perform this beautiful ballet.

Do higher-value checks fly less well than those less expensive ones?

Is there a link between the check ballet and the type of food consumed?

Does the check for the steak and fries try to woo the check for the little green salad?

Who else is watching this show apart from me?

Has anyone else even noticed it?

▶□◀

Daily Report

Seen on the noticeboard of the food court: "Daily Wisdom." The intention, no doubt, is to help us forget our Daily Boredom.

Seen on the checks in the food court: "Magic Number: 3225." I need to find out what magic there is contained in this number.

2 large coffees, 3 mini croissants, 1 mini pain au chocolat, 1 expresso.

Charrette

▶□◀

International corporations all go through what are known in France as periods of "charrette" (literally "carting", as in, "horse and cart"). When working with colleagues overseas, it's important to explain what is meant by this useful little expression.

In order to explain properly, one must understand whether this term is used to imply:

a) the idea of diligently pulling along a cart, and that you are some sort of tired donkey chained to a heavy load that you have to pull up a hill while you sweat buckets.

b) the idea of how much cargo is in the cart, and that it should be full.

c) the idea of pulling the cart in the right direction and delivering it to the desired destination.

Answer: none of the above!

Here's where it really came from:

"Oh! These charrette nights never seem to end! Endless evenings in the studio, where in unison we would sing songs, each one more indecent than the last, just to keep ourselves awake. But why charrette? Because the next morning we would have to use these little carts to transport our work to where it was going to be exhibited, and students who were a little late would still be working on it as they moved.

So we have the expressions "travailler en charrette" (cart working), "être charrette" (to be carting), "une charrette" (a carter). The works were delivered to the Chief Warden, Monsieur Lafournière, who was the kind of man that seemed like a gruff army General but he had a big heart. Mr. Lafournière knew how to command the respect of his students, however if ever the time came when they needed defending, he'd do it with all of the conviction as if they were his own children.

The exhibitions were in the mythical and grandiose 'Salle Melpomène'. It was a room that boasted relentless zenithal lighting that better served the exhibitions. There would be around 300 pieces of work awaiting judgment there. This kind of rigorous confrontation and the rivalry it created (among students) constituted the most crucial elements of architectural education."

So there you have it. That's exactly what it's like working in a multinational corporation. All of these projects with fancy names and in competition with one another, piled haphazardly into a tiny old cart, being worked upon as it moves along. And the mythical, grandiose room where they're all going, the Melonman Room (or whatever it was called), with its zenifluous (sic) lighting, the global market. All stacked up, ready to be presented to Monsieur Laugh-or-neigh. What if he was the one to be presented to the baying crowd of the global market? The guillotine would await him, I suspect!

So is the intense rivalry, and the colossal amount of wasted time that arises from it, integral to the continual functioning of the organization?

Daily Report

Oops! A personal email was blocked by the firewall and rerouted by the administrators who thought it was SPAM. Just what I needed. 1 call.0 chats (COMPLETE isolation today).Emails and emails and emails and emails...

€2.51 left on my card for the food court.Started up my PC at 9:42 am, shut it down at 6:17 pm. Did ctrl-alt-del eight times, computer crashes: zero.

Traffic

▶□◀

The movement of people inside a skyscraper adheres to some well-established rules.

Morning: morning people usually arrive before 9:00 am. At this time, the world belongs to them. They're the ones who switch on the lights. They connect the part of the world which has not yet woken up to the part which is yet to go to sleep. Everything is calm. In wintertime, it's still dark outside and there are little lights that glow, just as they do in each of the offices within the Big Skyscraper.

9:00 am – 9:30 am: Everyone else arrives. There's a lot of noise and chatter as they wait for the elevators. As I mentioned earlier, in order to minimize the amount of time people spend in elevators, the floors within the building have been organized into sections. People are also organized according to which section their floor is in and they may enter the elevator when their section is called. There's a lot of hustle and bustle involved in this separation of peoples, but with their "morning energy", they're more than up to it. Their faces are rosy and fresh. As soon as the doors open, you're hit with the sweet smell of coffee and perfume.

9:45 am – 12:00 pm: Big calm. If, by any chance, you happen to be walking around the building at this time, you'll notice that between one section and another there is little movement. The network and the servers are all busy, struggling to keep up with the demand. Information buzzes, beeps, and whirs along the cables, pinging from one server to another. We talk to each other with an electronic filter in between us. What happened to real conversations? To actually meeting someone? Now we just walk along with files underneath our arms and a cellphone glued to our ears.

12:00 pm -2:00 pm: Empty stomachs head downstairs. Cliques are made and broken during lunch break. You can learn a lot just by watching people as they walk to the food court. My gawping eyes stare in amazement as I count the amount of pink ties and gray suits. What happened to all the other colors in the rainbow? The stuffed bellies make their way back upstairs. Eyelids flutter upon tired eyes, despite all of the coffee ingested; a few shirts and ties have new stains upon them: "God damned f***ing ketchup!"

2:00 pm – 6:00 pm: The Big Calm descends once again. See 9.45 am – 12:00 pm.

6:00 pm – 8:00 pm: Tired bodies and eyes. Can't wait to get home. Frantic journeys to pick up the kids, have dinner ready on time or be at the theatre before the show begins. See you tomorrow for the same again. Faces are red and dreary. Ties have been pulled down an inch or two, suits and skirts are creased, shirts have been untucked, and the scent of perfume isn't quite as sweet as it was before.

After 8:00 pm: Face almost falling off. How did I get to this point? A day swallowed by work; the large multinational corporation stuffed full with your efforts.

It's dark outside. The Big Skyscraper is illuminated by a thousand little flecks of light; one in each little square. The tower is pleased with its day's work. Its stomach purrs with content. We have been digested with ease.

Yesterday's Daily Report

1 meeting canceled due to excessive daydreaming (I was so within my own thoughts that I went to the wrong meeting room).

0 vocal messages (heard "You have no new messages" 21 times. The female robotic voice has a cruel tone in her delivery).

3,265 passages of English to Franglais, then to French back to English then Franglais again. I don't know what language I'm talking anymore.

Changing Pastures in the Land of Skyscrapers

▶ □ ◀

When you change office (and building), you have to get used to moving frequently back and forth between the old and the new for a little while, kind of like a type of corporate changing of pastures. At least, that's what just happened to me.

I should explain. The giant company that I work for is so big that they've had to colonize multiple skyscrapers in the vicinity. There's the small one, which, to be fair, isn't really a skyscraper at all, just a regular building. Then there's the Absolutely Massive one (the one I'm sure one day will take off into space). There's the medium-sized one, inside which no one has any idea what happens. Finally, there's the Brown Tower, where I used to work before changing to the Absolutely Massive one, before returning to the Brown Tower. Still with me?

When your office is in the Absolutely Massive Skyscraper, you're in the same one as the big bosses. This is where you'll find the most people. Just like a beehive: all of the workers near to the queen. That's why the Massive Skyscraper has absolutely everything you could ever need in a workplace, and all of the meetings in which it's in your interest to be seen take place there. Basically, you go in there in the morning, you leave in the evening and you've hardly moved anywhere at all in between. Self-sufficiency. In the Brown Tower, there are far less people. And so there we all went, fairly regularly, to the Absolutely Massive Skyscraper which rules the world.

I warned my shoe repairman that he was going to make some good money from me. Just walking across La Défense to get work is enough to destroy a pair of heels in no time at all. The paving slabs aren't even correctly aligned, meaning you catch your heels in there ALL the time. It's for that reason that you'll see plenty of women walking along looking at the floor, hunched over trying to make sure they don't slip between the cracks.

Everyone has their own technique for getting from one skyscraper to another. You find that out along the way when you meet your colleagues who have also had to make the arduous journey.

• You've got the donkey technique, which involves taking your PC on your back, files stuffed into your rolling suitcase, and more papers under each arm.

- Then you have the chilled out transhumancers who take with them only the simplest of outfits, namely a suit with a tie flapping in the wind and their nose pointed skywards.

- Then there's those people who prefer Diet Transhumance. This type of tower switcher tends to travel lightly, tightly gripping only one sheet of paper.

- There are the busy ones who have no time to spare for anyone else, let alone themselves. They may choose to speed up their commute by using an electric scooter.

- Then there are the ones who are always late. They run while looking at their watch and talking into the cellphone that they're holding between their shoulder and their ear. "I'm gonna be 10 minutes late. Can you let Mr. Schmo know that I'm on my way and that I'll be there in 5? Thanks a bunch."

- You have the sporty types, who squeeze in a jogging session to their transhumance. These people need to be organized, because no one wants to see someone arrive in their sweaty t-shirt and old jogging pants just as the meeting is about to commence.

The great thing about switching towers is that is gives you the opportunity to escape. Ah yes! The ancient art learned in school of how to skip class! So you take a lil' detour and head straight to the mall to buy that new perfume you wanted, some sexy underwear, the diapers for the little one, a bar of chocolate or to the shoe-repair guy to fix your heels!

Daily Report

2 messages on my landline.

2 calls on the landline, 1 of which a wrong number.

Saw 2,561 colleagues in gray or black suits. 1,250 blue ties, 1,000 pink, 300 dark red, 11 yellow.

1 expresso, 1 green tea, 1 piece of Turkish delight. Note to self: box almost empty.

Stared out of the window 18 times to daydream.

Average temperature in my office = 52°F.

Need to remember to measure the thickness of my new carpet.

Vacation

▶□◀

It's completely calm in the Massive Skyscraper, and everywhere else in the city for that matter. That's because we're in the middle of August, and in France that's when everyone goes on vacation. Everyone. Either that or the computer servers have decided to go on strike and stop transferring the oh-so-important messages we send each other from one end of this little planet to the other.

The silence is almost worrying. It's during the vacation period that I'm able to smash all of my personal bests in terms of efficiency. I send out files by the thousands to those fortunate enough to be out of office. My own inbox is inundated with "Sorry, I'm not in the office right now. I'll get back to you as soon as I return."

Tomorrow I'm going to be moving out. Again. Once more I'm being moved to a new, temporary office. I find it kind of reassuring in a way. The day when they inform me I'm going to be moving to a permanent new office is the day I'll start to worry. When that day arrives, I know that they've finally decided where to store me inside of this giant cuboid. Where they're going to let me fossilize for the rest of my days. My professional days, of course.

Daily Report

Almost got stuck between the 15th and the 16th floors. 3 days now without a coffee. Not bad. Almost at withdrawal stage.

Summer "Works"

▶□◀

During the months of July and August, the word "work" takes on a new meaning. At least it does in certain parts of Europe.To slow down, to become motionless. Summer work actually means very little work at all.

"Summer works" means maintenance of the major highways and train lines that surround the capital city. Just when you think you'll be able to get from point "A" to point "B" faster now because everyone has left on vacation, you find out that it's most certainly not the case. In fact, now, in order to get from one place to another, you're forced to take as many detours as is conceivably possible.Then, if you do somehow manage to eventually make it to your office, you are suddenly struck by the deafening silence of the place. Then you're struck by the lack of emails in your inbox.And if you should dare to write an email yourself, you are met with a barrage of the aforementioned emails that look something like this: "I'm not in the office from the XX/XX to YY/YY."

Damn. How am I ever going to make any progress on this iTeach project?

Slowly but surely, you begin to give up. The lack of mails in your inbox matches the lack of any in your outbox. Less people call you than before. Your calendar is empty except for pointless meetings, which at least fill some time. Time, which now ticks by so slowly it seems like it has been stretched. And so you become bored. You need to find a new way of working. You've done it before, after all. Summer work also involves a lot of clearing out and general tidying. It keeps you busy enough.It has never been so sunny (except occasionally between the downpours). It's scorching hot. Burning. One starts to dream of past vacations, of ones that are yet to come, of ones colleagues in flowery bathing suits making sandcastles on the beach with their darling children. Ah! Finally something amusing to think about: the board of directors in flowery Speedos (I bet that's a sight to behold) building sandcastles!

Well, it was like that before smartphones were invented anyhow.

▶ □ ◀

Summer Summary

0000 voice messages, 2 emails per day (1 of which is spam).

1/8th of my cardboard box sorted (no need to rush).

0 flowery shorts seen.

32,658 times I imagined eating an enormous ice cream.

326,589 I imagined what it would be like smell the sea instead of carpet.

Moving Out Day

A little while ago, my ex-boss told me out of the blue in the middle of a totally different conversation that I was going to have to move offices. The office is the cuboid place where I live, breathe, work, where I spend all of my god given time working for this giant multinational corporation. Yep, this is where I spend a certain amount of hours, sat on a spinning chair in front of a computer that connects me to the entire world, making my neurons work so that I can send emails, engage in chats, and make phone calls in order to begin, to end, to lead and co-lead projects that have names that are basically impossible to pronounce.

If we take B as the lowest point and H as the highest, I spend hour upon hour of my life within BxH. Brrrrrrrr! It's enough to send shivers down your spine.

Getting back to the point; I'm changing cuboids. This is the national sport, the favorite game to play both within the Massive Tower and between towers (because remember, the giant corporation has many towers: Big Ones, Very Medium Ones, Little Ones, Black Ones, Gray Ones, Grayish-Black Ones and Blackish-Gray Ones). In nine years I worked from within 18 different cuboids. I counted. On this occasion, I'd been in the same one for almost one entire year. And no one wants that to happen. I'd made myself at home. I'd even stuck posters on the wall. I was beginning to grow roots from my feet into the office floor. This is simply not permissible. And so it was time. I had to move on.

So I started to wonder: what if they put me in a room shaped like a cone or a pile of sand, just for a change (and yes, the shape "pile of sand" exists - take a look in your old geometry textbooks, you'll find it)? How about a rhombohedron? Anything but an elongated cube.

I knew I would be in for a disappointment.

They moved me to a different side of the building. This meant that I had a completely different view and I'd no longer be able to see the sunset from behind my desk. That made me pretty sad. Oh well, I think the view should still be nice anyway, just in a different way. As usual I'd have to move mountains of files and documents with names like "Project Flim Flam Pt. 29" or "Filey McFilerson, Review 14.01", that I've frankly NEVER opened but that I keep nonetheless, if only for sentimental reasons. You just never know.

As you know, dear readers, not so very long ago, not everything was done electronically. I still have paper documents among my treasure trove that prove beyond any doubt that project Whoseit wasn't so terrible after all, while project Thingummy was a veritable rehash of something tried many times before. All of these little gems are filed away in colorful folders ready to be unearthed just as soon as anyone asks for them. And I will not hesitate, when the time comes, to get them out. And then immediately put them a new filing cabinet.

I said "hello" to the CEO and he said "hello" back.

I need to remember to measure the thickness of the carpet in my new office to see if I've been promoted or demoted.

0 boxes emptied.

Tidying up my mailbox: holy moly! At the same time, I'm trying to manage 20 projects. I'm struggling.

102.4°F: the temperature of one of my kids at 3.40 pm, grandma informs me.

24: the number of confirmed participants for the global meeting to discuss Project Thingy.

4: number of meeting rooms reserved "just in case".

2: number of European and Global meetings I have to organize on the same day.

0141065213: Doctor's phone number given to grandma.

Don't get the numbers mixed up... please don't get the numbers mixed up...

Company Conference

▶□◀

Large Multinational Corporations often hold annual meetings so that upper-middle management get together and discuss important matters, such as the mega new strategy that they would like to see implemented. And of course, they need to tell us what this strategy is, so that it may be implemented.

A few weeks ago, one of these very meetings was held for the highest ranking managers of the Franco-French branch of the Large Multinational Corporation, which I am still part of.

I was elated to find myself surrounded by my compatriots and to finally be able to speak my native language. Due to the immense number of high ranking managers at the meeting, a very large room was required to welcome us all. Rows of seating, a large stage, on one side a courtyard and on the other a garden. It was like being at a show. Everything was blue. Blue is a relaxing color. It soothes the soul. There were giant screens everywhere, and everywhere you looked there were big bosses: in front of you, behind, on each side... you couldn't escape them.

And there, a small figure on the large stage: The Big Boss himself. Even better, on one of the giant screens, there was the Very Big Global Boss, who obviously was not able to be present.

Everything was enormous: the numbers, billions of statistics that represented the incredibly large production output of the Large Multinational Corporation. I felt so small in comparison to these large, bloated statistics of my Very Large Company. And so we received a nice pat on the back: we're wonderful, we're great, we're doing a fantastic job, we are simply incredible people to work alongside. They spoke about passion, pleasure, and how everything is just won-der-ful. Then about how big we are, the biggest even, and we may even get bigger. Hmm. Perhaps it's futile, but something to think about: what if one day we just, you know, stopped trying to get bigger?

Conventions give you the opportunity to see a real smorgasbord of bosses:

- the unfunny ones (often the overwhelming majority).

- the one who keeps saying he's about to finish but keeps talking.

- the one who tries to be funny (an overwhelming majority).

- the one who keeps saying "if the situation improves, things will get better."

- the one who has come armed with an encyclopedia's worth of bullet point slides.

- the one who talks about promoting diversity within the board of directors, while surrounded by the board of directors who are all white men, graduated from the same school and are all about the same age.

- those who NEVER smile (it's a way of life: never smiling makes you look more important.)

Everything of course is presented in a way so as to at least try and make it a little bit interesting for the audience. Mention must be made of the excellent guest speakers, whose appearances served only to make management's presentations seem all the more boring and insipid.

Of course, it's very important to do all this, and I applaud big corporations for spending so much money on these meetings. They also give me the opportunity to see nice old colleagues that I haven't seen in a long time (and to carefully avoid others).

But please, only once a year. Thank you.

▶□◀

Daily Report

Blank. I invoke the right to stop counting on the day of the annual meeting.

Short-haul Business Trips

►□◄

Short-haul trips are ones that take you to another capital city within 2 hours by high-speed train or 1.5 hours by plane. Longer than that is medium-haul, and if you're going to another continent, it's long-haul. If you have a short-haul trip between European capitals, then you are 'Eurocommuting'.

Today I've got a Eurocommute on the agenda. That means a 6 am, break-of-dawn wake-up. I scurry down to the nearest Big Station. At this time in the morning you see two types of people in the subway: ones like me (except they're men, mostly) with their rolling suitcases and... an air of being very important indeed. Then you've got your Average-Joes and Janes; the general public, usually of a slightly darker skin complexion, off to their early morning job, working on a high-rise construction site, cleaning a high-rise building or opening up a high-rise building. That's the current state of Diversity & Inclusion here. It's more like Discrimination & Intolerance.

Once you arrive at the Big Station, you blend in with the mélange of these two different groups, along with the homeless folks who have come to warm themselves up, happy (or perhaps merely content) to have survived the previous night's freezing conditions. At the Big Station, everyone is moving in a different direction (each one with their rolling suitcase behind them making a "zuiiiiiii zuiiiiiiii" noise). Trains depart every 3.5 minutes. It's all rather exciting, especially watching the people who are running very, very fast to try and catch their very, very fast train, desperately wondering if they'll make it on time. Such a cruel early morning.

You get on your high speed train at high speed. Inside the carriage you find lots of men with lovely ties, dark suits, a shirt that's either blue, white or light pink and... an air of being very important indeed. In front of them is their mobile phone, their laptop and any other gadget that might give them an air of being... important. Sometimes you might find them in groups of two or three, and, if that's the case, they may have an air of being even more important than usual. The high speed train hurtles at very, very high speed into the very dark night. It's a funny sight, these carriages full of people who find themselves very important, dressed in their dark suits speeding headlong into the dark of the night.

Clickety-clack.

"This is your train manager Walter and I'd like to wish you a very warm welcome you on board blah blah blah..."

Clickety-clack.

You arrive at the Big Station of the big European capital which looks curiously like the one you've just left. A bustling crowd of taxi drivers holding up signs awaits those passengers from first-class who arrive with their rolling suitcases. People who have a very important air about them don't have much time to waste. Because they are, after all, very important indeed.

There's a lot of traffic in the Big capital where you've just arrived, just like there was in the Big capital you just left.

10 am: Arrive. Work. Make progress on the Thingamajig project.

4 pm: Leave. Expect traffic all the way to the Big Station.

5 pm: Back on the train that goes very, very fast. People's faces looking less fresh than before. A few of them relax a little, others keep going and continue typing frantically on their laptop's keyboard. This relentlessness is exhausting.

Clickety-clack.

"Ladies and gentlemen, we're sorry for the slight delay. We should be moving again sometime within the next week or so..."

When you finally arrive, it's a struggle to actually get off the train because the army of cleaners who are getting on don't have much time to do their job, because, after all, the train that goes very, very fast needs to leave again very, very soon.

8 pm: Home sweet home.

By my calculations: 7 hours of travel, 6 hours of work (including breakfast). Does that seem reasonable?

Daily Report

Encountered 542 very important men indeed with 542 rolling suitcases.

Traveled 638 miles at a very, very high speed and 2 miles very, VERY slowly.

Heard 542 mobile phones ringing.

Listened to 542 conversations that I really could have done without.

Medium-haul Business Trips

▶□◀

A medium-haul trip is one that takes over an hour and a half to fly to from where you live. Medium-haul trips begin, of course, with a very early morning. The first serious question to ask yourself is: "am I going to participate in the company-wide effort to reduce expenses, a new, permanent policy of the Large Global Corporation? Because if you want me to contribute, the only choice I'm left with to get to the airport is via public transportation. The problem being that when you're embarking on a medium-haul trip, that often means a 7 am flight from the airport, added to that the half hour required for check-in, and fifteen minutes "just in case". You're looking at being at the airport by 6:15 am, minimum. That means getting on the 5 am train from my place, with one change. Great.

That's why your willingness to take part in the Large Global Corporation's new permanent effort to reduce expenses is not exactly full of enthusiasm; especially when you take into account the extra 15 minute that you can gain in bed. So, taxi to the airport it is. The reservation is made the night before, with a priority password, naturally.

The first wave of joy washes over you as you see there is no one else on the road. You get to the airport early. Plus with the extra 15 minute "buffer zone" you gave yourself, you're actually REALLY EARLY. One must remember, however, that between the hours of 7 am and 7:30 am, scores of flights take off from here, departing to each of the four corners of Europe (of which Europe has none). The airport is bustling with people. You are led to the automatic check-in post. And of course, you are surrounded by the "sssssshweeeee, chacka-chacka-chacka, chikree chikree chikree" sounds of the little rolling suitcases that are positively buzzing with the thought of just... getting on board. Each one of them so proudly displaying their little red "Cabin Baggage" label

Sometimes there's a strange mix of tourists wearing flowery shorts and businessmen in suits and ties, with their business class ticket clasped in their hand (they always have the side where it says "Business" showing, because everyone must know that

they are indeed part of this class of traveler. They are not the same as the people in Economy).

Going through security: getting completely naked is a real possibility here. First it's your jacket, then your belt and shoes (and that lonely moment when your realize that your socks have got holes in them). And yep, damn: beep! "Sigh. It must be my necklace." Beeeeep! "Darn. My keys." Beeeeeeeeeep! "OK, I have no idea. Maybe it's the wiring in my bra?"

A little moment to get yourself dressed again. FYI I didn't remove my bra... I mean seriously, c'mon.

In the terminal. I admit that am no longer a picture of tranquility when flying. I'm afraid of lots of different things. In fact, I have very vivid imagination when it comes to possibilities of things happening: diversion, engine failure, defective landing gears, loss of thrust at take-off, horrible crash during take-off or landing, a fire caused by an idiot smoking in the toilets. If there was one place that I didn't feel half scared to death, it was in the airport. Until the collapse of the Terminal E, this thing that was supposed to be a demonstration of the genius of French architecture. Ah well. That's the way it is. Fortunately, in Terminal F, which is not a supposed to demonstrate the genius of French architecture, there are less risks involved. But still. I still spend time pondering what could happen. Ah well. That's the way it is.

OK let's go. It's time for boarding. At 7 am you are bound for the four corners of Europe (of which I remind you, Europe has none). You'll see your friends (of course they are, I assure you). Just one last coffee and we're good to go.

Daily Report

1,500 airmiles on my loyalty card from this business trip to Barcelona. Hell yeah! Well, really it's just an imaginary pleasure. I'll never actually use them.

60 loyalty points on my bank card for having used it to reserve the taxi. Another imaginary pleasure. I'll never be able to actually use them. When will I get loyalty points for public transportation at home ?

It's 7 am and already one coffee has been downed.

D for Depression

F*****g Depressing day, even though I was wearing my very colorful jacket. It wasn't enough.

There's a terrible atmosphere in the Big Skyscraper. The elevators are broken; they shake as you're going up. Depressing.

Didn't even see anyone new or interesting in the elevator just so I could daydream a little about all of the colors of life. Depressing.

I went upstairs to polish the soles of my shoes on the soft carper of the big bosses. Depressing.

I have no idea where I should start with the Thingummy Project. Nor the Whatchamacallit project. Or the Whoseit Project for that matter. Depressing.

I decided to go for a walk across the pretty footbridge in an attempt to provoke some kind of deep, serene thought. Closed due to slippery surface. Depressing.

The new Flippityflop database is ready to be rolled out. Server GB100 went down just as they were sending out the announcement email. Depressing.

The US3000 didn't manage to solve the problem. Depressing.

I broke the heels on my shoes while walking across the damned paving on the esplanade. Depressing (well, not for my shoe repairman).

I had to leave earlier than usual to pick up my sick child from school. The stench of vomit welcomed my arrival. Depressing.

I haven't had time to prepare for the super-duper, incredibly important call tomorrow. Depressing.

I finished the day washing clothes, bathing the kids and preparing dinner. Depressing.

I won't have an Internet connection for one week. Depressing.

The front page of today's newspaper:

$W+(D-d)*TQ/M*NA$ = The Most Depressing Day of the Year.

That explains everything.

"Traditionally, Monday brings with it a loss of energy and the feeling that you are losing control of what's happening. The blues are at their worst the last Monday of January, which is itself the most depressing month." Depressing.

To depress: from the Latin "deprimere: to press downwards from above." And that's exactly what's happening. I'm being pressed from above. And in the middle, there's just mush. Soaked in alcohol, now all that's needed is to set me alight and watch me go up in thousands of tiny multicolored sparks.

But there's no one here to light the fuse. Depressing.

Chin up. The Moon was EXTREMELY beautiful this evening.

Daily Report

325,665th day locked in the store room down in the basement for the woman who tells us how many messages we have on our answering machine.

102,879th day trapped in the orbital for the woman who tells us how many messages we have on our cell phone.

1 invitation to lunch received.

2 congratulatory emails for my contribution to the global project.

D for Depressurized

▶ □ ◀

Wonderful Depressurized day. I wore my amazing coat of many colors, and the world was a beautiful place again.

There was an joyous atmosphere in the Big Skyscraper. The elevators passed each other; they glided up and down with ease. Depressurized.

I met a handsome man in the elevator and I lost myself in the magnificent ocean of his eyes. Depressurized.

I polished the soles of my shoes on the caressing carpet of the Big Bosses' floor. So, so soft. Depressurized.

I made start on all of the projects I needed to without thinking any more about it. They seem to be going well and heading in the right direction. Depressurized.

I went to get some fresh air on the pretty footbridge they've built in the middle of nowhere. Closed due to danger of slipping. Ha. I could have hurt myself. I decided to walk across the Grande Arche while I was outside and admire the view all the way to the Arc de Triomphe. Depressurized.

The Huzzamcwump database is back online (we've only been waiting one year for that to happen). Depressurized.

One of my children has fallen sick. I have no meetings scheduled so I can go and pick them up without any problems at all. Long live autonomy. Depressurized.

My kid was so happy so see mommy during this hard time for them. Depressurized.

A nice hot bath and a good dinner (prawns in clementine juice, invented there and then). Depressurized.

Planned cut-off of the Internet. I'm going to make a detox cure. It will do me some good to be off it. Depressurized.

The front page of Le Monde:

$W+(D-d)*TQ/M*NA$ = The Most Depressing Day of the Year.

Phew. It's in Great Britain. Not here. Depressurized.

Depressurize: all of the little pixies with big, ocean colored eyes which light up the sparkles in my head.

In the end, everything is just a question of perspective.

Daily Report

Flippityflop database is operational. Champagne!

1 call with the big boss setting up the new totally awesome project; he's OK with what's presented. Excellent.

1 big coffee, 2 small coffees.

In order to not get cut like a sausage when entering the Big Skyscraper: present your badge and then wait (in your head count until 2 ¾ seconds), then move forward in a smooth, casual manner.

Reply with History

►□◄

Reply with History is a function that enables you to reply to an email and leave underneath it the entire thread of the conversation that has happened so far.

It's incredibly practical: it means that along the way you can add new participants in your grand quest to find an answer (to the question – because in general, these emails always begin with a question). And so you end up having long email chains that are absolutely gigantic in their length. Some people say that certain email chains have been going on for years (centuries-long email threads are not yet possible), which get longer and longer each day, meandering along an unknown, never-ending path. What if one day these email chains managed to escape from the servers and came to try and strangle us?

Can you even imagine a time before emails existed? How did we ever keep track of things? Balzac and Madame Hanska, for example, wrote to each other for years, each time posting both their reply and the previous correspondence to ensure that the recipient may follow the conversation with ease. That would mean they would have posted their letter, along with the previous mail, and the one previous to that, and the one before that too, until it would have become simply absurd.

Looking at it more positively, this function allows you to be sure that you haven't lost your interlocutors; that everyone is able to follow exactly what is going on (with regards to a question that everyone is probably interpreting in their own way) just in case they need to. And if, perchance, someone, somewhere attempts to actually tackle the answer to the question being posed, well, that might just be too much for the server to handle.

Daily Report

2 voice messages.

3 text messages.

Traffic on all of the line

Clickety Cla... "Our train has stopped." Oh great, thanks! I hadn't noticed! "We'll let you know what's happening when we have more information."

What exactly are the possible outcomes when a high-speed train stops?

- You arrive late

- The train starts moving again

- You change route

- The train turns around and goes in the other direction

- You arrive very late

- The train starts moving again... but backwards

- You never start moving again

- You arrive very, very, VERY late

- The train goes to another destination entirely

One thing is for sure: you can't overtake the train that's in front of you (a train that is also supposed to be traveling very fast) which has ... stopped... in front. A traffic jam of high-speed trains.

As soon as the fateful announcement is made, everyone puts guess what to their ear? Their mobile phone! PCs stop their tippy tapping.

And one more thing, while we're on the subject. Don't get out your mobile phone as soon as this happens (and – especially - don't have it glued to your ear). No one wins in that situation. If everyone takes out their phone at the same time, that network also becomes jammed. The train has stopped, and there's nothing anyone can do to change that fact, so you may as well just chill. You still don't know yet whether you're going to be late, very late, very very late, or perhaps you'll even arrive on time with a couple of seconds to spare. You may as well just wait to find out. That's what I did, and I found out that the outcome for me was that I was going to be very, VERY late indeed.

Finally, we've arrived at our destination, Brussels. And guess what? More problems: "We're sorry ma'am, it's going to take you a while to get where you're going. Everything has been completely blocked off." Protests, strikes... basically a load of people who'd like to retire at 58 (crazy - I thought we only had people like that in France). Then the subway is closed because people are on strike. Take a deep breath, chill. The problem is that I was supposed to have a conference call at 9:30 am with Paris and Milan from here in Brussels. At 9:30 am, I was still at the train station. As in, I wasn't at the office. I had no other choice but to join the conference call from the taxi. A truly HORRIBLE experience.

"Erm... Angeline, it's great that you could join us, but we can't hear anything now you've connected to the call. Thanks for making the effort, but really, we can't hear each other now. You're breaking up. All we can hear is like a crackling sound an.. krrrrrkk pssssssssh fweeeeeeee."

OK guys, fine. It's really not worth the effort. When I arrive I'll reconnect. If there's still time, I mean.

Finally arrived at the office. A bit of luck: the elevators are working again. They're moving fluidly between the floors. I managed to join the call five minutes before the end when the most important elements were being discussed: what we need to do and who's going to do it.

61 supposedly high-speed trains not moving.

Smiled at 26 people (it's the only way to keep up the morale in this crazy world)

Drank unknown liters of Belgian coffee just to keep going.

362 blue ties seen at the Belgian office, 8 text messages received.

Saw 526 spreadsheets on 526 different brands of PC on the train (numbers keep you busy).

Stopover

It's the magic of time. In a time which plays with time. And distance.

I'd traveled thousands of kilometers in just three days. Before leaving again, I had a short stopover at home. At least, what's left of it.

You take off. A few short hours later you land, further away. Each time you arrive, you notice that things are just the same as back home, and completely different at the same time. There the same because there are still human beings, living, breathing, doing business. They love, and they suffer. Me, I like to look for the things that make us different (except for the language). It also needs to be acknowledged that economics has guaranteed that a large city is always a large city.

I have plenty of anecdotes regarding this subject. Some wonderful, some less so. That's because, thanks to my job in the Large Multinational Corporation, I've been lucky enough to have the opportunity to stay in some places that I would never had paid for myself.

So there you are. Just a few thoughts. Nothing more. While we're here.

The Merger

Large Multinational Corporations have a complex: they're not large enough. It's clear that they are not managed by women. Otherwise, it would be the opposite, for sure. Women always want to be smaller. They want things to be slimmer, lighter.

Given the fact that the majority of large firms are indeed controlled by men, they want to always be bigger; bigger than their neighbors. So what does it do? Or rather, what do they do? Well, they merge. The verb "to merge" is quite beautiful. It can invoke thoughts of two loving bodies coming together as one. But then again, you might also think traffic lanes merging. And I can tell you, when two large businesses merge, it can result in an enormous wreck. A bad experience for both parties.

Sensitive souls, leave now.

Low blows are allowed in this sport. Get out of my way, I'm here now; this town ain't big enough for the both of us.

I'd just like to remind all of those companies that wish to grow forever larger, that in Aesop's fable of "The Frog and the Ox," the frog meets an explosive end.

Boom!

Size of the large international corporation before merger: 5,300 units.

Size of the large international corporation after merger: 8,900 units.

The "Galette"

▶□◀

The "Galette des Rois" is a type of cake that is eaten by Christian tradition in France (and other predominantly Francophone nations) on the occasion of the epiphany, on the 6th January. Often, this tradition is played out at our places of work. Hidden inside the Galette is a small lucky charm, and whoever finds this charm gets to wear a golden crown and choose who his or her queen or king will be, respectively.

Despite all of the pretty little nicknames given to it, the Galette des Rois is a tradition that we are obliged to partake in (rather than one that we choose to). But why, oh why, are we forced (or do we force each other) to eat a stupid cake at work?! We don't make pancakes on Candlemas. I've never seen anyone roast a turkey at work either, for that matter. So why do we give this cake the special treatment?

As you've probably guessed, I've had the pleasure of partaking in this lovely tradition. Although it was getting toward the end of January and we'd pretty much gone passed the acceptable window of time.

So my team and I were invited to participate as some kind of "extras", because we no longer belong to the group of so-called "local teams" (we are an international group now, you see). It was a heavy atmosphere. Like, really heavy. Heavier even than the nauseatingly sweet interior of the cake, drowning in butter, now that I think about it. Only about one-third of the people turned up. All the others were no-shows.

The cherry on the cake was obviously the boss' speech. He's not actually our boss anymore, but you know, we went anyway to make up the numbers. There's currently a horrible atmosphere between each of his teams, so keeping the mood light was not going to be an easy task, even with cake. The boss began his speech by saying it wouldn't take much time, or, at least, less than last year. Generally, when something begins with an announcement like that, you know you're in for the long haul.

When you're in a situation like this, you must avoid, at all costs, making eye contact with one of your coworkers. This will prevent you from bursting into a fit of giggles and laughing yourself to death (or back to life, depending on your perspective). So we were lucky enough to be given an update on what's happening throughout the department, each and every person in the Big Skyscraper was congratulated for their efforts and we were generally told how totally awesome we all are. He did still end his talk with a nod toward the future, of course. As expected, we heard all about how to "turn a negative event – the planned firing of half of the staff – into an opportunity".

I left hastily, feeling a little disgusted as I thought of the words the words from one of the classics:

"Je suis la galette la galette...

Je suis faite avec le blé, ramassé dans le grenier

On m'a mise à refroidir, mais j'ai mieux aimé courir !

Attrape-moi si tu peux !"

"I'm the galette the galette...

I'm made with flour, gathered from the granary

They put me to cool down, but I preferred to run!

Catch me if you can!

▶□◀

Daily Report

Almost fell asleep in the middle of the afternoon after a wave of fatigue hit me out of nowhere. Fortunately, I had the galette there to perk me up.

I feel very proud when I check my dashboard and look at the activity in all of the countries that I'm responsible for.

And another thing: I wonder how many miles you would cover by going around all of the floors in this tower that isn't round?

A Prawn's Destiny

What an amazing destiny for this prawn! I need to say that the story I'm about to tell is most likely about a baby prawn. Or if not, it was an adult prawn but from some sort of dwarf species, if such a thing even exists.

Once upon a time, a baby prawn was swimming around somewhere deep down in the ocean. The little animal was enjoying exploring warm new waters, finding new places to have fun. He wasn't alone, either. He was swimming merrily along with his shoal of other little boy prawns and girl prawns. One day, a boar came along and threw a fishing net right into the area where these happy little prawns were playing.

Our baby prawn died of suffocation. Baby prawn was brought onto land. Baby prawn was frozen and put into a box. Baby prawn was transported in a big truck. Baby prawn had his shell peeled off (well, actually I'm not really a prawn expert so it's highly possible that the shell was removed before being frozen and not after). Either was the result is the same, and the incredible fate of this prawn is not affected in any way.

Baby prawn was thawed by putting him into a pan and stir-frying him alongside lots of little vegetables in lots of pretty colors. Baby prawn was put in a plastic box and covered with a sheet of aluminum foil. Then he was put into another truck. And the end of his long journey is drawing near.

Now it was time for a high-speed take-off into the air. Then a long wait. A long wait until he was over the coast of Croatia. Airplane food. Baby prawn is placed before me. Ready to be eaten at 35,000 feet above the Mediterranean Sea.

Really, what a remarkable destiny...

Daily Report

Angeline Vagabulle

Paris, London, Brussels, Athens, Rome, Madrid

Sounds pretty chic, right?

Serious fatigue

▶□◀

I had lunch today with a colleague, with whom I've also been friends for many years. Since college, in fact.

While sat eating, I suddenly had a flashback. He was currently going through the exact same thing that I was around two years ago in the Large Multinational Corporation. The uneasy feeling about globalization; feeling like you're going down blind alleys and not knowing about what's really going on in the organization. Badly defined boundaries, inexistent rules, projects that were unclear, people fulfilling roles that didn't mean much, tasks that were unimportant, and the people who were there living this. It was a feeling kind of like "what am I doing here? What am I contributing? What am I really doing, flying to the four corners of the world?"

How did I get to where I am? I planned, I clarified. I mean, I tried to. I set things up, I put together a team. I mean, I tried to. I made things happen, I communicated. I mean, I tried to. I networked, I slid on the carpets with my soles (or the other way around). I mean, I tried to. Most importantly: I moved eight times (six times professionally-speaking and twice personally) which I always tried to avoid doing, but eventually I had to give in without having much choice in the matter.

So you're probably wondering what I have to say about all that now, having explained that I went through the same thing two years ago. If I'm still asking myself the same questions, such as "what am I contributing?", "what am I really doing, flying to the four corners of the world?" Well the answer is no. My mind is clear and calm on these matters. I don't want to know anymore. I don't feel the need to try and understand anymore. I've stopped interrogating myself. I move forward and I watch with amusement this little world which I am a part of, always keeping busy and making sure I don't have any time to spend reflecting on these types of questions.

But I admit that it's tiring. And thinking about it, today a colleague asked me what they should do to not feel so tired. I suggested that they should engage in activities that are not so tiring. Stop thinking so much, pretend like you have had a lobotomy. After giving him this advice, the conclusion he reached was that he need to buy himself a television!

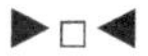

A nice little moment during the day

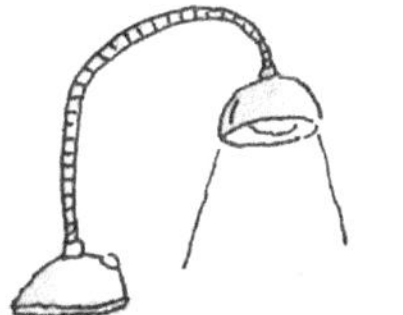

...when the guy from maintenance came to screw in a new lightbulb in my desk lamp. He pressed the button and it illuminated all of the papers on my desk with such splendor ...

Kafkaesque Hallucinations

▶□◀

This is the story of a little invoice that didn't arrive in the right place at the right time. Poor thing. So we weren't able to pay it.

But I really wanted to. I promise. If I'd had the company checkbook, I would have signed the check a long time ago! But these days we try and simplify everything. So much so that even paying an invoice is difficult; even impossible.

I'll explain.

The sender of the invoice was a company called Lambda, which was based in the United Kingdom. They sent their (paper) invoice in mid-July. It was sent "for the attention of Angeline," Angeline's address, the Big Skyscraper, Land of the Gauls. The invoice arrived on Angeline's desk while she was on vacation. When she returned from vacation at the end of August, she didn't have time to even put her feet on the carpet, before she was being called left, right and center (then left again) for one thing or another. By mid-September I find the time to stamp the invoice "To be paid" and to forward it to accounts (the people who look after the checkbook).

Tick-Tock, Tick-Tock. Time passes...

Beginning of October. Strange. I still haven't received confirmation for the payment of the Lambda invoice through the invoice base. What's going on?

Hello, anybody there? Mrs. Accountant Lady? Ah well that explains it, Karen McWotsit's on maternity leave. And nobody told me. And of course she has no replacement so her mail is just stacking up while her colleagues are dealing with it as best as they can.

End of October. Boom! The Lambda invoice has finally been validated on the invoice base. How do I know this? Because I receive and email telling me so, of course. Thank goodness for technology. But now it's my turn to be out of office again. I'm somewhere right in the middle of nowhere. I've got my smartphone with me but I have no access to the company Intranet. Only my emails. So it's going to have to wait a few more days, the famous Lambda invoice.

Beginning of November: I'm back in the office and finally have access to the Intranet. Damn. I can't validate it because "You have exceeded your level of authorization," I'm told.

I send an email to accounts: Help! help! SOS! What do I do?

The invoice is forwarded again by accounts via the invoice base to the Big Boss for validation.

And that's when it started getting a little more serious (because before that it was actually quite funny).

Mr. Bingley (who comes from a country somewhere north of France, whose precise location I won't divulge) comes down on me hard (in the language of the country to the north of France): "What? The Lambda invoice still hasn't been paid? What's going on?! This is a big, BIG problem!" To give you the short version of the story, since the beginning of November I received at least three emails per day asking me about the situation regarding the Lambda invoice.

At the same time, I've got the Big Boss within our side of the company who is taking all the time in the world to resolve the situation. He has sent 425 emails to 425 different people looking for an explanation as to the origin of this invoice, should it be approved, if it was budgeted correctly and if it was accounted for before closing. He gave me the third degree in order to be absolutely, totally, positively sure, sure, sure that we can indeed pay this f***ing invoice for a few thousand Euro, that I have already explained 56,432 times was submitted before the deadline.

Beginning of December: Big Boss sends out an email asking for the invoice to be validated by a guy who works on the big, big global accounts, who in turn does like everyone else has before him: asks me if we can indeed pay this invoice.

Should I reply? Long live technology, and all of the wonders it has done to simplify this type of management task.

Daily Report

I almost lost my entire shoe because my heel got stuck in between the paving stones of the "Esplanade de la Défense".

2 coffees, 1 tea.

Chats, emails, calls, emails, chats, calls, calls, emails, emails, blah blah blah...

Kafkaesque Hallucination: The Sequel and... The End ?

▶□◀

Tuesday morning: received an email from Mr. Bingley (very angry): "Are you crazy? This is absolutely unacceptable. We simply cannot tolerate having such a delay in payment."

I reply with an email which doesn't exactly make the situation advance in any way, but feels good nonetheless.

I understand Mr. Bingley. But this poor little invoice is still stuck somewhere within the multi-level system.

At this point, a sort of domino effect occurs. A Big Boss, who was in copy for Mr. Bingley's email, replies and asks another Big French Boss (the one who has been preventing it from being validated for the past X number of days) "what's going on?"

Now for a perfect demonstration of blatant hypocrisy: "everything is fine," he replies. Seriously, screw you, coward. I validate the invoice at 10:43 am.

10:44 am: Second email (this time it's for me): "I can't validate the invoice actually. There's a problem. The system is telling me that I don't have the right level to authorize it. "Angeline, can you sort this out and make sure we put this situation to bed?"

I'm strangling myself. The invoice had been sent to him in the first place because I'd had the same damned messaged a month and a half ago. Now it's me who is seriously annoyed. After all that we're back at the beginning. I call for urgent help from my colleagues who were holding the keys to the safe: please, please, please, we need to get this done.

And so they did it. By validating the invoice themselves. Why didn't they think of that sooner? At least now I know. Time to get out the champagne! I got confirmation Thursday that it had finally been paid. Well, in truth there was one last step in the process that needed to be done electronically, but once that was confirmed we were home and dry).

So it was a happy ending. The invoice self-destructed within the system and Mr. Bingley received some little numbers somewhere in his account.

▶ □ ◀

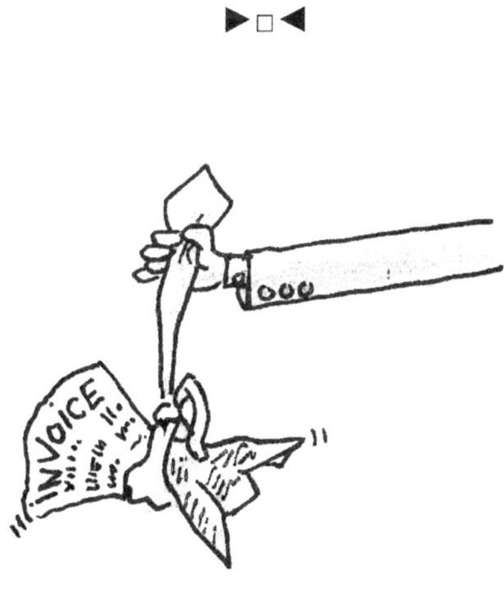

Daily Report

A moment's thought for all of the little invoices stuck in the unbelievably inefficient new system that was set up to boost productivity in the already-too-big Multinational Corporation.

"All Lines Are Busy"

Angeline is French (that's me) and she is on the very fast train that travels between Brussels and Paris. Angeline is traveling with K (Belgian), S (Spanish), MJ (Argentine-American), A (Luxembourgian), and F (French, living in the UK). GG, T and M, the handsome Italians, have taken the plane. Angeline, S, MJ, K and A are traveling second class. F is traveling in First Class, a privilege earned through working for the global organization. This means that F is in another, more comfortable coach, but it's important to note that the First Class coach does not actually travel any faster than the Second Class). Kaa is Greek and has just arrived in Paris.

We begin a GSM call in Paris/Athens/Paris/somewhere between Brussels and Paris:

"Hi, Angeline, it's Kaa on the phone. How are you?"

"Oh, fine thank you. Where are you?"

"I am in a taxi. In Paris. And I have a problem. I have the name of the hotel but not the address. Do you have it?

"Yes. Sure. Just a minute."

Fast, fast, fast! Lots of talking between K, A, MJ and S in a mix of French and English (I don't speak

Spanish, or Luxembourgish). Kaa is lost in Paris. We need to give him the hotel's address that's written somewhere on a scrap of paper. Shoot. We found the name of the hotel but not the address.

"Wait a minute Kaa. We are looking for the address. I should have it on my computer."

I connect myself to my computer.

PC working. Opening emails. Damn, I don't have it. I must have archived the email that contained the address. PC working. Opening email archive. Damn. No address there either.

I disconnect from my PC.

We start another GSM call between Paris/Athens/somewhere between Brussels and Paris:

"Kaa, we can't find the address. But wait a minute. F surely has it. But she is travelling in another coach. I need to call her. I will text you the address."

We begin a new GSM call somewhere between Brussels and Paris Coach 8/Paris/London/somewhere between Brussels and Paris Coach 2:

"F? It's Angeline. I'm calling you because Kaa is in a taxi in Paris on her way to the hotel but she doesn't have the address. You wouldn't have it, by any chance?"

"Yes. Two seconds," – papers shuffling – "here it is." 113 rue Strapoufard.

"Oh! Thank you so much." I knew that F would have the address. She's super organized, F. Not like me at all (not like K or S for that matter).

Fast fast fast. Help Kaa out of her situation.

New SMS somewhere between Brussels and Paris/Athens/somewhere in Paris:

I send the address of the hotel from my French cellphone, while I'm somewhere between Paris and Brussels, to a Greek one lost in Paris. Message delivered.

Wow! What an adventure. It should be noted that no one was thrown out of the train, nor the taxi. My, how the lines were all busy that day.

▶□◀

Daily Report

2 text messages sent in English I need to improve. 1 reply (I think they didn't understand the other one).

I can't even count how many texts I sent in French (nor how many I received, for that matter).

4 meals served in a plastic tray in 4 days.

I've lost count of how many coffees.

Brand New, Never Used

▶□◀

"Integration: the technique of finding a function, the derivative of which is equal to a given function. This is indicated by the integral sign "∫," as in ∫f(x), usually called the indefinite integral of the function."

Err, no. Must be something else.

Ah, here it is: "the act or process or an instance of integrating, such as the incorporation as equals into society or an organization of individuals of different groups. See also: assimilation, fusion, incorporation, insertion, unification."

In the large multinational corporation, there is a particular period of time when new people are integrated into the company. This is often done in big batches. We open the doors at the bottom of the big skyscrapers, and we tell the little darlings to come in and see how wonderful it is here.

You always know straight away when there's an integration session going on. In the hallways people are constantly buzzing and fluttering around. In the canteen, in the food court, in the toilets. Young, rosy faced recruits everywhere. Their suits are too big for them or just really awkwardly-fitted. You can see that they still haven't totally got wearing a tie down to a fine art, and walking on heels is not yet something that comes without an awful amount of effort. In the food court, the pre-paid payment cards beep louder than everyone else's, or they just get stuck in the machine so everyone else is forced to wait around until the normal flow of people in line can continue.

The newbies always block the elevators, roam aimlessly in the long corridors and turn up lost in every corner of the office that they shouldn't be. They try their hardest to understand the files we send to them that are written in another language that they can't yet speak well, full of code words and acronyms, and round-up summaries presented as bullet points on almost-transparent backgrounds.

But most importantly of all, the thing which enables you to spot one of the newbies with ease, is their unrelenting enthusiasm. They still believe that they will flourish in this large multinational corporation; that they will actually enjoy themselves here. It's a challenge, there's always something to be done. With their open spirit, they'll be working alongside lovely people, each one of them happy also to contribute their all to the overall growth and wellbeing of the company. For them, everything is still just an innocent little game. They smile. They're all so polite, and they never, ever complain. I mean, they're... happy. They're more than happy to go on little short haul trips to some backwoods town outside of Paris with a stay in the Zip Zap Hotel just north of Sômeplace-sous-Bois.

This fresh air turns rather stale rather quickly. Within only a few weeks, they'll be assimilated, incorporated, unified (OK, you get it. See the definition above).

And with each new batch, we, the oldies (those of us who gallantly try to resist the temptation to fall into a deep pre-, pending- or post-project depression who are not helping the Whatchamacallit project to progress, nor really helping anyone else in the company to progress. At the end of the day, that's not really our job anyway) we wait and hope that maybe this time we will be welcoming THE batch of youngsters who will be able to reinvigorate the company, to get us out of this mess and just sort everything right out. Let us dream a little.

Maybe you were once part of a revolutionary new wave like this? Well, darn. What happened to us? Why did we ever stop?

▶□◀

Daily Report

22 text messages.

8 coffees.

The Friday Storm

▶□◀

Last Friday, the stability of the Big Skyscraper, within which the Large Multinational Corporation is located, was under attack.

When my coworkers and I all opened our inboxes this morning, we could hardly believe our eyes.

So last Friday I was actually on a little business trip (short haul) and so I wasn't in the Big Skyscraper. While I was away, a tremendous storm hit Paris, bringing with it strong gusts of wind that bellowed unforgivingly against the tower. It was one of those storms that was so fierce that it reminded you of what a small, pathetic little species of ants we really are when faced with the universe and the elements within. It was so strong that flights were canceled, trains traveled at half-speed and cars were doing the same. We were basically experiencing the same fate as the characters in Ravage by Barjavel. And for hours and hours afterwards, many well-informed people within the media were able to tell us that "basically, there was a lot of wind. Really, quite a lot. And it blew really hard, and stuff, like, started flying around." It was really quite interesting to hear how wind works.

And so what about the Big Skyscraper, you ask? A tall tower like that is planted firmly in its foundations and stands proudly against the elements, so there's nothing to worry about, right? Wrong! The tower was actually moving. So they decided to send around an email to reassure everyone. Here is the actual email they sent:

"A few people working on the upper floors of the building say they can feel the tower moving. The structure of the building was designed to withstand such strong winds. There is absolutely nothing to worry about."

Hilarious. First of all, the people working on the upper floors are the directors. Think about it: as the tower moved and creaked they must have thought that the end was nigh: a revolution, the inevitable anarchy that would ensue, rules being broken with abandon. When a director asks a question, someone had better answer. And so the explicative email was sent. It was the wind's fault.

The thing that I don't understand is how it can move up top but not at the bottom. If I understand correctly, it's all about the resistance and the flexibility of the materials that you use that would have been

chosen to stand up to these types of forces. It's pretty reassuring to know the Big Skyscraper has been built to withstand strong winds. I mean, they might have forgotten to think about it. Imagine, the first little breeze that blows, the tower is blown into the sky. Plonks itself down on the Moon. Or boom: onto the ground. No such luck.

So there you have it, the cherry on the cake: there is nothing to worry about. Everything will be alright. Rest assured. Stay at your work station. Go back to sleep. We will take care of you. "Trust in me," Kaa said to Mowgli. Reminds me of when they said that the big boat would never sink. Remember what happened next?

So in conclusion: "Blow wind, blow!"

Daily Report

Windspeed = 2 knots (so nothing to worry about).

Exterior temperature = 47°F (no risk of the tower melting).

Beautiful Music

▶ □ ◀

Match the sounds to the words below: phone ringing (landline), jingle of a computer starting up, email notification, noise from the office door opening, chat notification, squeak of chair turning, phone ringing (mobile), printer/photocopier working, smartphone mail notification, text message notification, printer/photocopier jamming, computer shutting down.

diloudilou diloudou

shtonk

brzbrzbrz

shtonk shtonk

Voulaoup ettchac ettachac etchac

ouip

diloudilou diloudou

ouip ouip ouip

brzbzzbrzz

shtonk

sloumpf vroumch

Miaouhhhh

Voulaoup ettchac ettachac etchac schplurf

shtonk

dilou louidilouididloudilou

Tink tink

Miaouh

bzzzzzzzzzzzzzzzzz

crouinchhhhhhhhh

shtonk shtonk shtonk

Miaouh

ouipzzzzzzzz

pfloutch

Ouizzzzzzzzzzz

iiiiiiiisnooooouuuuuuuuu

Ahh... the sweet music that comforts me in the office each day.

SILENCE !

ETTACHAC
SHiiiiiiou
SCHOuii
zink-TINK-zink
BRTINK.
ZBzzBRzz
iiiiiiilllisnooouuu
ETTACHAC
ouip ouip ouip ouip ouip
Brozzzzrzzarr
CRRRR
SHTONK
SHHHH
PLEASE KNOCK
BEFORE YOU ENTER!
TINK
TINK
TINK
TINK
shtonk
shtonk
SLUUMM...
ouizzzzzz
doudi
dilou
dilou
dilou
doudi
ouizzzzzzzzzy
RENARD

Daily Report

Shut up!

My Buddy

▶ □ ◀

I have a buddy who also works in the Massive Skyscraper, like me. But there's quite a difference in what that entails for each of us.

The first difference is that we don't work in the same place. He works more in the background, in the rumbling belly of the Tower. He works to ensure that others have a clean stage on which they can perform within this big theatre. Truth be told, it's thanks to people like him that we are able to have any kind of life in the Tower that, if we're really being honest, is not that bad.

So my work buddy is Mauritanian. We became friends because he'd often see me working late on the Gronkatok project. As for him, he comes to work when everyone else is supposed to have gone home. He's the one who vacuums the carpets so it can still go "shui shui" (well, not the carpet on my floor. It's far too worn to go shui shui anymore). He's the one who empties the trash cans that are full of waste paper. He's the one who cleans your desk so that when you arrive in the morning, everything is sparkling clean and shipshape.

I don't see my buddy very often, because I usually finish my day earlier, so it was quite unlikely that he would become my friend. My office is always locked, too, so my buddy was never able to enter. So that evening, he was happy to finally be able to clean the mysterious, inaccessible desk that was hidden away inside. Well, to be honest, it wasn't terribly easy for him to clean anything on that desk given how much stuff there was on it. Having said that, there really wasn't any dust to clean, due to all of the papers protecting the surface.

In the end, we got to know each other. "Hey. You here tonight? Still not finished?" So we got talking about Mauritania (he was astonished that I even knew it, and could even tell him the capital city) and blah blah blah and blah blah blah blah. I told him that I'd previously done some training with a Mauritanian lady when I first started working at the Large Multinational Corporation.

But the day that my buddy really became my buddy was when he made me laugh until my sides split.

I was in the Big Skyscraper's food court carrying my tray, wandering around having a look at what's on

offer and trying to decide what I should have for lunch. Suddenly, I hear a little "Bonjour!" And there he was: my buddy. Ready to serve me whatever the hot dish of the day happened to be. I was a little taken aback to see him there. "You work here too at lunch? You never take a break?!"

We chatted a little bit more later. I felt like I should. It's modern slave labor on a grand scale. We sit upstairs, desperately trying to motivate ourselves to make progress on the thoroughly boring Whatchamacallit project, but we should be under no illusion that we are paid rather well for it. On the other side of the fence, my buddy works for hours and hours, doing tasks for which he is neither thanked nor rewarded, for an equally unrewarding salary.

I digressed a little. My buddy. I started seeing less and less of him because they made me change floor and even tower. But whenever we do see one another, we always have a little catch up to see what's going on in our respective worlds.

What if we could do something to rebalance all of this?

Daily Report

2 boring meetings.

8 uninteresting slides.

3 coffees.

564 pink ties.

The Great Update

I arrive this morning and walk into the tower. I place my foot down once again onto planet Large Corporation after the small parenthesis of a weekend. As I'm waiting at the bottom for an elevator to arrive, suddenly it hits me: I don't have a computer. I just remembered, before leaving Friday I left it with IT to be updated. The stress gripped me: being at my desk without a computer. I mean, what on earth was I going to do without a computer? No connection to the world? OK, better go and find it.

I got the little beast back and everything was very neat and clean. How nice of the guys at IT to have done that for me! I start it up, a little worried. What if I can't connect to the world? Phew. It works.

OK, so what exactly has IT done with my computer?

* At start-up, instead of going "Pa papa", it now goes "Ta pa poom."

* The icons have changed shape and color.

* When I deleted an email before, there was a little blue dot. Now there's a little cross.

* As usual, there are loads of icons that appear in windows that I have no idea what to do with because I still only use the same few programs that I always have

since Windows 3.1 (I've made some progress though. When I first started it was version 2.11.)

* There are now both horizontal and vertical navigation bars that enable you to go from one place to another faster than ever before (virtually speaking).

* When I transfer an email from one folder to another, it actually MOVES it.

* When I'm choosing the recipient, the window that opens is prettier than before.

* In checkbox lists, now there is a little square to click to make your selection. Before there wasn't.

Basically, there were loads of little improvements that all made life that little bit easier. The colors were more vivid and, most importantly, everything ran a lot faster. That's EXTREMELY important. Now I can do everything at a greater speed than before. The one thing that it seems no one has considered is that the human brain can only go so fast.

Daily Report

I'm going to put a sign up in the toilets reminding everyone that we signed a climate protection agreement that commits us to fight against global warming.

Thickness of the carpet on my floor: 1/10 of an inch.

Thickness of the carpets on the Big Bosses' floor: ½ an inch.

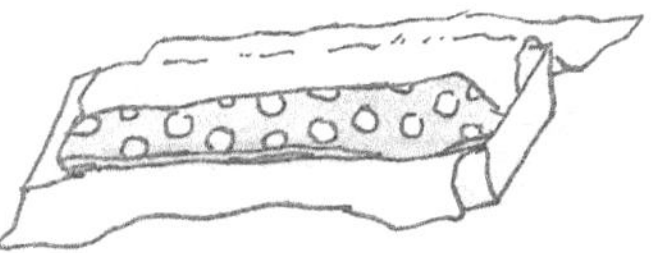

1 VERY elegant colleague not wearing a tie (hold on, wait...)

0 male colleagues wearing a red suit with yellow polka dots.

Visibility

▶□◀

Every idea needs a visible envelope – V. Hugo

▶□◀

If you want to do well in a Large Multinational Corporation, you need to know how to be visible. Not just anywhere, though. You need to be seen where it counts.

That could mean:

* Being in a very important meeting. But watch out! When I say you need to be present, first of all it means to be there physically speaking. But your brain must also be there. BOTH brains. The right AND the left. But that's not enough. Far from it. While you are there, you must make sure that you are not hidden in any way, for example behind a colleague, or dozing sleepily at the end of the room in silence. You need to know the right moment to speak up and that is when you must drop a comment that is so unforgettably marvelous that whoever is managing the Whatchamacallit project will never forget you were there (N.B. make sure that you choose a meeting where there is indeed an important project being discussed; that reduces considerably the amount of meetings that you need to attend, you will soon come to realize).

Don't contribute too much, either. That could be annoying.

* Participating in a conference call: basically the same principle as the meetings. Once you find one which fulfills the criteria detailed above and you've entered into the call, you need to be a little bit strict with yourself, for example you must stop reading your emails, close all of your chat boxes and stop browsing the Internet. Just sit down and put your coffee on the table. Generally, conference calls last around one hour (anything longer than that and you can guarantee no one is listening anymore), and say what you need to say at around the 45 minute mark, after the usual blah blah blah that begins such calls.

* Play the long game. This is important. There's no use waving your arms about in the air to get yourself seen (or sending loads of emails, or talking endlessly). There are so many other people doing the same thing that in the end, you just become another lost voice in the crowd.

* Recently, a colleague of mine has been getting a little bit too enthusiastic about the need for me to become more visible. Do I look like an idea that needs an envelope? OK, fine. I shook away the cobwebs, and went upstairs to polish the soles of my shoes on the carpet of the Big Bosses. "Hello, hello," big smile big smile, "my name's Angeline, I'm in charge of the Whoseit project. I decided to take the initiative".

I can already sense the questions from the most profound and complex among you: "What good is it anyway, being visible?"; "Why do you want to be seen?"; "What good will it bring you?"; "You being visible isn't going to change the world, is it?" And of course, a popular French saying: "To live happily, one should live hidden."

Let's finish this up: If you want your place in the sun (i.e. to pass along your ideas), well, then you're going to need to be visible. See above for how to achieve this.

"But what good does it do, passing along your ideas?"

It makes them visible, of course.

▶□◀

Daily Report

Invisible.

Nomination

I'd like to give fair warning to the sensitive souls out there: this chapter is going to be deliberately sexist.

I was recently appointed to a new role within the company. There's no reason why only men should have their appointments announced, but if you should have any doubt as to which of the genders receive the most coverage, open up your daily newspaper and count how many female appointments are actually written about. About half of the toes on your left foot should suffice for the task.

So when I was appointed, I decided to let people know about it. Modestly, course. No giant billboards. Just enough to make myself visible. And whaddya know? Soon after, I arrive at my desk one morning and there's a letter from a recruitment agency called "Femmes & Carrières. " As I opened it, I thought to myself "Wow, it seems like finally my status as a woman who has a career within a large multinational corporation is finally being recognized. "Women" and "career" are not mutually exclusive concepts.

I read the letter. It made me fall off my cushion (rather than my chair - I now sit on a cushion on the floor. It's safer). The aforementioned agency was writing to me in order to suggest that I might now be in need of an assistant. That's when everything suddenly became clear: whenever a man is appointed to a new position, he gets an assistant, usually female.

So that explains why I might be receiving such a letter myself. Obviously the career this agency is alluding to for women is one of an assistant to men who squat in the position of Director.

Ugh. Ugh. And ugh again. I'll let you know what they say about these lovely assistants: "She will be your first source of support: facilitating your everyday tasks, she will take care of your agenda, organize your meetings, business trips and take care of your accounts should you be absent. Perhaps you have not yet found the pearl to help you to solve your logistical problems? (sic)." I'll stop here before I vomit. They're really, truly offering me a young woman to look after me: a wife, nanny, mother and confidante, all in one. Just like these men have always dreamed of having.

So I put it to Femme et Carrières: for me it would be a male assistant to do all of my logistical planning. But I don't want one anyway. In any case, you'll need to adapt your marketing spiel for women. Women are coming to work, not just as assistants, and they're going to change these stale old ways of doing things.

Daily Report

Heard on the esplanade: "It's not just the KPIs we need to look at, but also how they're calculated." You can say that again...

I changed my voicemail message. To change your message *4#22#enter your passcode#56#3#1*87#you can access#you are happy*confirm#69#your new message has been confirmed.

2 large coffees (in the sun, so good), 1 small coffee (in the sun, so good), 1 beer (in the sun, so good).

Open Sesame !

▶□◀

The following story is VERY loosely based on real events.

▶□◀

Passwords guarantee security within a company.

Different types of passwords exist:

- The password that gives you access to a domain or network

- An http or Internet password

- The lock screen password which doesn't have any other name

- Program passwords: email program, program to manage your global employee profile, program that gives you access to the databases

It's important to know the difference between a good password and a bad password. And remember: a password is your first line of defense against unauthorized access to protected information.

So let's go over the bad passwords, which must be avoided at all costs:

- Your first or second names, in any form: as it is, backwards, written twice, letters rearranged

- The first or second name of your husband, wife, boyfriend, girlfriend, lover (if you have one) or children

- The name of your pet, someone in your close family, your neighbor or your BFF. Take note that I said "your pet" first

- Your social security number, your car's license plate number, the name of the street you live on (you can apparently use the number, however)

- Any information about you that is easily available to others, such as your birthday (your bra size and the brand of condom that you use don't make the list of things not to use)

- Passwords with the same number or letter used repeatedly (but how will the airheads manage?!)

- A word that can be found in the dictionary or any other list of words. Not sure where you would find a list of words that can't be found in a dictionary

- A password with fewer than six characters: no explanation, it's just like that

- The title of a film, song or book. Boohoo. Another reason to dream taken away from me

So now that I no longer have the right to use any real words for my password, what am I supposed to do?

So here's the right way to create a good password:

- It must have both CaPiTaL and LoWeRcAsE letters.

- Preferably, it should have at least one lowercase letter, one capital, one number and a symbol. It's going to be tough to find a word with all that

- The password should have eight characters. OK, there's something wrong here. Words with seven letters must be pretty unhappy; six or less is not OK but eight is. So what about seven? No way.

- Choose a password that you can type without having to look at the keyboard, and that people cannot read by watching your fingers type. I know sign language but not finger language. I guess you learn something new every day. The thing is, typing a password that fulfils all of the criteria above, without looking at the keyboard, well, that's going to be tough. It's going to tie my fingers in knots – not pretty. Maybe I'll be compensated for an accident at work.

- Use a password that's easy enough to remember that you don't have to write it down: this is a good one. A complicated word that fulfils the above criteria that can't be written down and you need to remember it by heart. Not easy.

So, if I've understood correctly, I need to remember a password that will look something like this: a!M2rsW or mCdL&8jP and I need to learn how to type it without looking. And of course that would be too easy, so I have to change this "word" every three months; and I can't use the same one within a year. Nightmare.

Of course, if you enter your password incorrectly five times within 30 minutes (meaning once every six minutes) well then you are permanently locked out and rejected from the system. That's actually quite tempting. The system is so thoroughly unwelcoming that I actually think long and hard before I even decide that I want to enter.

Me, I'd prefer each morning to type something a lot prettier when I connect to such a thing: abracadabra littletutu pointy hat lotus flower. I think it's a lot better, don't you?

Daily Thing

85-ds_(flazlèà7(UYRvcpp&'xlAOOGDE is my new password.

The Virus

Bad news. The Large Multinational Corporation has put a firewall in place in order to prevent the interior network from external viral attacks. Great, except they forgot to create an antivirus that would protect us in case of infection.

To this end, the ghastly stomach virus against which I'd vigilantly protected myself managed to spread. I watched it get passed from office to office. When it realized it had been identified, it decided to take revenge. It got me. So it started yesterday right in the middle of a meeting, and it arrived firing on all cylinders, so to speak. Apparently, it liked me as a host. It decided to make me its new home.

The trip to the nurse's office was interesting. A little 19th century, they were extremely courteous and ready to send me home without hesitation. Kind of like the school nurse. They take great care of you (makes a change) and give you lots of different pills in many colors to help you get through it all: "Promise me you'll take yourself home. Your health is more important than work."

In the end, I was so under the influence of what she'd given me that I somehow found myself typing away at my keyboard as usual until 6 pm. The view from my office was more magnificent than ever, on the other hand.

It seemed like the journey home took forever...

▶□◀

Daily Report

I shook the hand of the CEO! What if it was him who made me ill? Or maybe I gave it to him!

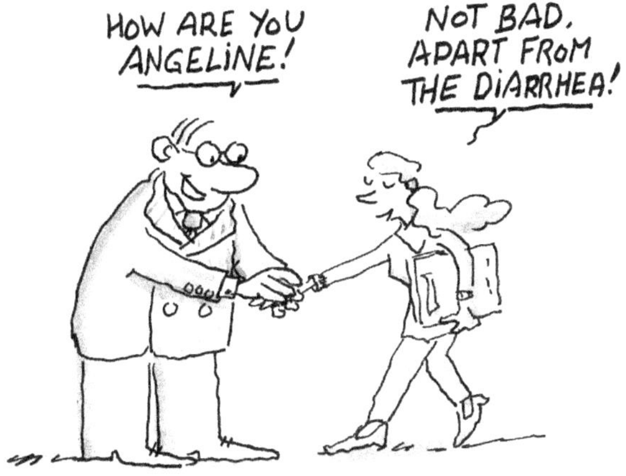

The carpet on the Big Bosses' floor has gotten thicker: ¾ of an inch.

Thickness of the carpet in my new office: 1/10 of an inch in the center but just less than 1/4 an inch around the edge of the room.

8 coughing fits.

10 mins nap at the nurse's office.

102.6°F when I got back home.

Rude Little Photocopier

▶□◀

OK, so let's be clear here. The erotic story that I'm about to tell didn't exactly happen with a photocopier. Nope. The motor that I'm going to talk about (because we are talking about a motor) is way more complicated than the kind of simple photocopier that I had used when I was younger (a debutante, a mini Angeline in the scary new world of the Multinational Corporation and when I spent a lot of time at the photocopier).

Nowadays, photocopiers are multifunctional. And now, due to their additional features, they're also much bigger. They take up a lot of room and make a lot of noise: whirr, buzz, click, clack...

The primary function of the machine though remains to make photocopies.

Now however you can do one-sided "simplex" (from a one-sided document), one-sided, double sheet (from a double-sided document), double-sided "duplex" (from a double-sided document), duplex (from two single-sided documents), back page, stapled, unstapled, double stapled, bottom stapled, top stapled, grouped, ungrouped, mixed, A4, A3, A5 (A5 only in theory though, because there's never any paper that size loaded), blown up, shrunk or mirror image. All of the different options were enough to make me dizzy. You could even combine the functions, for example a mirrored duplex stapled recto-verso ungrouped document. Wow. Yeah, let's give that one a try!

But it doesn't stop there. The photocopier is now also the printer. And it too has a lot of functions. One-sided (from a one-sided document), one-sided, double sheet (from a double-sided document), double-sided (from a double-sided document), double-sided (from two one-sided documents), back page, stapled, unstapled, double stapled, bottom stapled, top stapled, grouped, ungrouped, mixed, A4, A3, A5 (A5 only in theory though, because there's never any paper that size loaded), blown up, shrunk or mirror image. Does all that remind you of something?

Back in the day, when I was a kid, if a machine like this broke down, you had to wait for days before some maintenance guy came along with his red toolbox to fix it. Things aren't like that anymore. The machine is now able to repair itself, with the help of a "user oriented" digital display and help program.

Usually, it begins with a big sigh from the machine.

ohhhh arrrgh naaaah

You look at the tiny little screen and see that the machine is trying to communicate with you:

"Incident in Zone B. Open the main panel." What that really means is: "Something's itching me in Zone B. Take off my shirt."

So you open the main panel.

Sigh. Arrrgh naaaaah

"Pull green handle 2" is displayed on the tiny little screen. That's when you're supposed to put your little mitts into the belly of the beast (what that machine wouldn't do for us to have a little fiddle with its delicate parts).

"Remove document from Zone 2." Erm. There's no document. Rude little thing, too.

"Warning, the zone might be very hot." OK come on, is this machine going to calm down? I have zero desire to fool around with a photocopier. It's not my type anyway. The muscly guy on the 31st floor maybe, but the photocopier? No way. Right, I'm closing it back up. The machine lets out another sigh.

Ohhhh naaaaah

Daily Report

3,256 mini power failures on the network.

Turned off the lights in the restroom 8 times.

2,159th day trapped in the 39th floor attic for the 12 guys who pedal on bikes to make the elevators go up and down.

Redundancy Package

A redundancy package. How exciting. I love packages! Nice little gifts, wrapped up in shiny paper and decorated with a pretty bow.

Not so fast. A redundancy package doesn't contain that nice little bracelet you saw in the store window while you were out shopping last week. No, no. It contains the details of your being fired.

There was a mass delivery of redundancy packages recently in the Large Multinational Corporation. One day, out of nowhere the announcement was made to those concerned:

"So, well here it is. Hello everyone. We've decided to hire a big jumbo jet to take 80 of you to planet unemployment, if that sounds like something you'd be interested in, let us know."

Hilarious. Except it's really quite a difficult procedure that you need to go through in order to charter the plane that will take you to a new job anywhere other than in the Large Corporation, with lots of deadlines, forms, papers to sign, and for once, no database.

Some have no choice whether they get on the plane or not. That's what gets everyone so stressed: what happens if not enough people volunteer? How will they decide who becomes a volunteer?

The calm before the storm.

They started accepting applications for voluntary redundancy on Friday 30th September. Maybe you'll find it hard to believe, but there were people who were so desperate to get on the plane they sent theirs on Friday at 00:01 am just to be sure they were at the front of the line, so to speak. I wonder if they managed to get a seat in Business Class.

Daily Report

Heard cardboard boxes begging to be emptied of their contentso physical letters in my inboxHow many liters of coffee will I have drunk by the end of my 40-year career? What happens in my office when I'm not there? Right now?

Now I understand why people ask for a parachute clause when they join Large Multinational Corporations.

Refusal To Board

I arrived merrily at the airport the other day, I can't say exactly when because I'm so busy with work at the Large Multinational Corporation that the days are beginning to become a bit muddled.

My cabin baggage rolled along smoothly behind me, swish-swish. Tonight I'll be somewhere else entirely. Somewhere sunny and warm. I'll be working in a dream destination; one of the lucky ones.

I make my way to the line and wait in front of the lovely white desk that's so high the only thing I can see is a well-groomed head poking out over the top of it.

Hmm, what's going on here? There seems to be a problem.

"Excuse me, could you tell me what's happening?"

"Yeah, basically the plane is full, there are no more seats for your flight to Athens."

"Sorry, what do you mean?"

"Seats. There aren't any."

"Sorry, what?"

"The AIRline..." (I won't mention its name here, but let's just say it's among the biggest in FRANCE) "...sold more tickets than there were seats on the plane. It's called overbooking, and..."

"Oh really? The BIG FRENCH AIRLINE WHOSE NAME I WON'T MENTION DOES THAT, DO THEY? They sell more tickets than they have places on the plane?"

"Madam, you see..." (no, no; I don't see) "...it means that tickets can be sold cheaper. Before, customers complained that the prices were too high. Thanks to overbooking, they are now able to reduce ticket prices."

"OK. But let's be reasonable. What's the point having a cheaper ticket if you can't get on the plane? It costs a lot of money to be stuck here on the tarmac!"

"Calm down, please."

"How are you even calm? Am I obliged to smile at this? You want me to hug you?"

"Don't worry, you are priority for the first flight that leaves tomorrow morning."

"Are you kidding me? The department who make travel arrangements at my company specifically told me they would book a flight for this evening because the one for tomorrow morning was full. And yet here you are telling me that there are places available. On top of that, the travel department told me that my ticket had been confirmed."

"Well, that's not the case ma'am. You're on a waiting list."

I enter a number into my mobile.

"Hello? Mrs. Thingy from the company travel agency? Can you just confirm to me that my ticket had indeed been confirmed? Because they're telling me that I'm on a waiting list."

I don't even know any more if buying a ticket guarantees that you'll have a place on a plane that will takes you thousands of miles away. I mean, who really knows these things anyway.

"Don't worry, ma'am. You are protected by European law, which states that you must be compensated." Ah great, that's better! "Here's a voucher."

The LARGE FRENCH AIRLINE WHOSE NAME I WON'T MENTION then pay for you to stay in a hotel and for dinner. How kind of them. What about my cancelled

meetings? Can they reorganize those for me? And how about the time away from my children, can they give that back to me?

I'd rather not go into the details of the terrible night spent in a hotel located right next to the runways of the airport. I can confirm, however, that on average, a plane takes off once every two minutes, even in the middle of the night. Now, I'm not an overly prim and proper or fussy person, but this was just awful. I slept four hours at most. At least it gave me time to brush up on my knowledge of "overbooking" and "what benefits I can expect from it" (yep, that's really how they describe it. That's good marketing, I can tell you.

Something to sweeten the pill, that makes you believe that it's fine, that life is good).

They say that it's necessary because there are frequently occurrences when people book a ticket and then fail to arrive for their flight. So it means that someone else can take their place. Well I say that the ticket has already been sold, and the company still keeps the money even if the person doesn't show up, so they lose nothing anyway.

And – you may want to take a seat before you hear this one – it also stops other people from making a reservation for the flight. I just don't get it. Between not being able to make a reservation, not going anywhere (because you couldn't make a reservation) and being able to reserve but not being able to go, I personally prefer the first option.

It doesn't stop there: they tell you that this is a way for airlines to minimize risk. For them, that is. Not for you. You, you're just a schmuck to them.

The airlines rely heavily upon statistics for their operations. And guess who is behind those stats? Computer programs that analyze statistical probabilities. Argh! I'm going to strangle myself.

OK. I stopped reading after the first page, as disgusted as I was at the situation, I realized that I was merely an insignificant piece of dust, fighting against a Large Multinational Corporation.

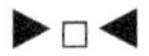

Daily Report

I hate the modern world (and Large Multinational Corporations).

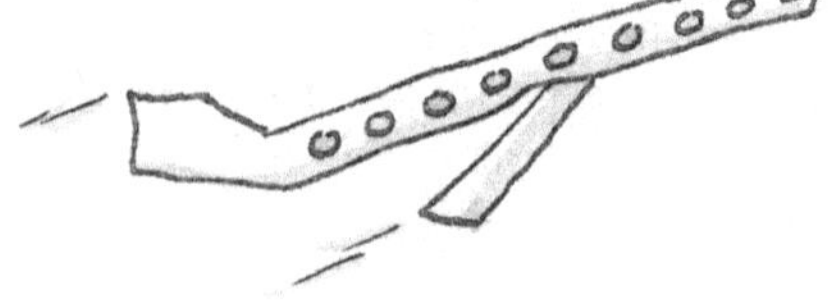

24/7

►□◄

The Earth is round. The Earth makes a full rotation every 24 hours. That means that there is always someone awake at moment T, and who is working. What am I trying to say? The result of this is that there is always someone awake and always someone, somewhere, who is working. It simply cannot and must not stop. Otherwise, the Earth will stop turning. It's a well-known fact.

The Global business league had just realized this and has decided to use it to its advantage: the Large Multinational Corporation will itself become an indomitable sphere of business activity.

Example 1: Just before I was about to move out of my house into a new one, I called my electrical supplier. Before the call ended, he said to me: "Madame Vagabulle, you can call us 24/7." I asked him: "Don't you ever sleep?" I heard a little sour laughter at the other end of the line. Followed by a very awkward silence.

Example 2: I'm about to be deprived of a night out for the third time in a row because of some reports that need to be finished at the Multinational Corporation where my partner works. I don't think the US team realizes that when they send something that 'must be finished by 6 pm', the deadline is for a time when we in Europe are getting ready to go to bed. One of the paradoxes of this ever-more globalized world is that now, thanks to all of its rules, we must give up our dreams. Quite literally.

Example 3: Conversation with one of my colleagues who has global responsibilities, a global team and global projects. "You know how good it is, having a team that covers three different time zones? The team is always working. Sometimes we get answers to questions before we've even asked them! It's genius!" Whoa...

How am I supposed to handle this, when I've got kids to look after? They aren't ready to handle a 24/7 lifestyle yet. Right when we're reaching the end of our day, the US team starts bombarding us with questions. Right when school's about to finish, or when we're getting ready to go to bed or get on with any other kind of nocturnal activities. Ahem. So the global report for Thingy can wait until tomorrow morning. Because

really, is there anything catastrophic that's going to happen if it's not done by then? Wake up (or rather, go to bed)! Let's be reasonable here.

Daily Report

Switched off the lights 32 times in the toilet (why does nobody switch off the lights in this office ?)

Woop woop! Database formula now auto-fills thanks to program developed by technical engineer that wasn't included in original system.

3 global projects launched (into the ether...)

SuperBusinessWoman

Lalala. Wake up.

"Mom, mom! I peed in my pajamas!"

"Coming sweetie."

First washing load of the day.

"Err, who's taking care of them tonight?"

"I can if you want."

"OK, I don't have a problem with that."

Smack. Crunch, crunch (breakfast)

Crashhhhhh!!

"Oh! My darling. Can you be a little more careful?"

Need to crawl underneath the table to clean up the mess. Darn, darn, darn!

Swimming stuff ready.

"Where's your blanket?"

Make sure you put the right suit on when you get dressed. In just a few moments, Supermom becomes SuperBusinessWoman.

Ok, done. Everyone's outside.

Chackchackachacka Chackchackachacka (the journey to work)

La la la, la la li (some music in the earphones)

Lilaloo stong stong stong (PC starting up)

Ding dong

"You know how to change the settings on the Bleurk database?"

"Err, you need to go to the settings in the form that's just on the menu when you open it up..."

Ding dong

"OK. I'll give that a try. Thanks."

"No problem."

Flip flap flop (sound of papers on the desk)

Clack (snapping the elastic band on the Bimble project folder closed)

Fweep. Read the email that just arrived.

"Could you provide me with the work your group did last week?"

Reply: "Yes. Sure."

Click (attach document).

"My pleasure."

Ring ring

"Hi Angeline! How's it going?"

"Good, thanks."

"Say, I'm just calling you because it seems there's some bad code in Pliffilly Duckface."

"Err... is there?"

Ring ring

"Hi Angeline! How's it going?"

"Oh! Yeah, good, and you? Time for lunch soon, huh?"

"Yep. Perfect!"

Buzz buzzzz

"Actually, can you take care of them tonight in the end?"

"OK."

Ctrl alt del (PC frozen). Meeting.

Ctrl alt del (PC frozen).

Ctrl alt del (PC refrozen). No time for this.

Lunch with colleague coming from abroad.

Slurp... Slurp... Lunch.

Blah blah blah. Meeting.

Ding Dong

"Hi!"

"Hi!"

"When will the Ladelswap project design meeting be scheduled for?"

"Err... In March. The 21st."

Ding Dong

"Great. Thanks. Bye."

"Bye."

Ctrl alt del (PC frozen).

Meeting. Blah blah blah. Blah blah blah.

Ctrl alt del (PC frozen).

Ding-a-ling-a-ling

"Hello. I'm calling you to remind you that your dance course will recommence this week."

Zwip zwip zwip zwip zwip zwip

The mails are coming in fast now. OK, let's do it. Invitation for a meeting about Twiddleythump, reply to a question, forward some other questions, delete, delete, delete (spam mail).

Oh man. I'm looking after the kids tonight. Need to work faster.

"Hello. Yes hi. I'm calling about the meeting tomorrow. What do I need to bring to it? Ah... OK."

Make PowerPoint slide in precisely five minutes (new personal record).

Ding dong

"Are you coming to the gym tomorrow?"

"Err... yeah."

Ding dong

"Hey. See you tomorrow."

Tap tap tap (dialing voicemail)

"Hey! It's me. Just to let you know that I'll be talking about Gruntlenoops, Dilly Dally and Cats on Wheels projects tomorrow in the meeting. I won't be talking about Duckface. If you want me to change anything... send me an email. Actually, just leave me a message. Or wait. Send a message to my mobile. Not the office. Bye.»

Attach document. Zwee. Mail sent.

Start/Shut down (always seemed strange to click on "Start" to stop something).

Right. Time to put on my rocket shoes.

Click clack

Read some files that I didn't have time to read in the office. What are we going to eat tonight? More reading of files that I didn't have time for. Where did I put my dance shoes? Read more documents that I didn't have time to read at work.

"Due to an accident 200 miles away from where we are now there will be significant delays for those traveling to wherever you're going. We apologize for the inconvenience."

Darn, darn, darn! But really, what am I going to eat tonight?

Buzzzzz

"It's Littl'un One and Littl'un Two's mom!"

Clank (Open the door. Wow, it's been repaired.)

"Mom! Mom!" Little people flying in all directions. "I made some little stickers." "And I drew a rocket." "Wow!"

Change costumes. Paint-stained tracksuit. Soft socks.

"Ahh! He hit me!" "I wanna watch Scooby-Doo!"

Dilingdiling

"Hey, how's it going?"

"Hi."

"You know the meeting on Friday? We need you there."

"Err... OK. Sure."

Time to fold the laundry. But what am I going to eat tonight?

"Ouch! He hit me!"

Tap tap tap (dialing)

"Hi. It's Angeline. Just calling to see if you could make the meeting on Friday, introduce everyone?"

But seriously, what am I going to eat tonight?

Sniff sniff. Ouch. Big hug.

Oh, my. We're going to die of suffocation under the enormous pile of dirty laundry, or if that doesn't happen, under the enormous pile of clean laundry waiting to be ironed. It's nice to have options.

But seriously, what am I going to eat tonight?

"Time to eaaaaaaaaat!"

OK. Done. Everyone go to bed.

Hold on. What did I eat tonight?

Daily Report

Couldn't even count the amount of emails, texts, calls and chats. We drink too much coffee. I'm managing too many things. Will this life tire me out eventually? What if I just stopped? In the middle of all this pandemonium, is there anyone who's actually thinking about me? Am I alone (well, along with the people who are reading this book) in feeling like I'm somehow going in the wrong direction?

Fighting Change

I'm not against change. No. But right now, I admit that I feel like here's too much of it. Or I must be getting old, because things seemed a lot easier before.

Now everything has been over-complicated. I think that my main grievance with the direction taken by the Large Multinational Corporation is that every decision is taken or every new strategy given the seal of approval only as a result of its financial implications, and nothing else.

For example, the new ZET database they introduced in the company.

Already, to get off to a bad start, I can't remember what ZET means. As usual, something has been made shorter in order to save time and money. Before, there was a simple tool that we used to make requests when we needed to reserve business trips. Nothing too complicated: you put in the date, the destination, then someone validated it, after the travel agency would make the reservation while respecting the very respectable travel policy of the company.

This all needed to be changed, apparently. It was too expensive. The people at the travel agency took up too much space. And you had to pay them. And you could never be sure that they were really buying the cheapest of the cheap tickets. So they had to go, naturally.

The basic principle of the new system is that you now have to do everything yourself, no agency to help you out if there's any problem or you're not sure what to do. You've not been trained in this, nor are you paid to do it, but don't worry about that. Because thanks to the Internet, you, the end user, you can do everything you want all by yourself with no problems at all.

I'm already lost on the ZET home screen. Thankfully the highly specialized designers of the new site that is going to improve the efficiency and profitability of the Large Multinational Corporation have taken the time to provide a user guide. 67 pages long. I mean, it's no surprise that this new tool took 11 months and 32 highly specialized developers working like crazy to build, test and implement. So, naturally the guide would take 67 pages in order to explain all of the sophisticated new functions on offer, thanks to the revolutionary technical innovations which speed up transactions, reduce costs, make navigation easier, reporting more user friendly, easier to read and that implicates the workers in its use (sic).

Now that you haven't read the guide (because the first line said that the tool was super-easy and "intuitive"), you enter the trip you need: Paris/London, for example. Easy.

There are 351 ways to do the Paris/London trip on the dates that you require. On a highspeed train, on a very chic airplane, on a cheap airplane or by car-ferry (this old way of traveling between France and the UK still exists. Why not just give me a motorized scooter). There's a very long list with all of the different options. You can go to London with CheapJet: except that when you arrive, you're 100 miles from London. Of course, you could take the very chic airline, but the Large

Multinational Corporation won't let you (they have no problem reminding you that it is possible, while temptingly leaving it there just to check that you really are as ethically irreproachable as they think you are. You can look, but don't touch).

OK, I'm going for the highspeed train. Only 32 options; I'm making progress. So I can take the seats on promotion (written in big, gray flashing letters at the top of the page to make sure that I don't miss it), which is, it's true, very tempting. Promo code for the offer: HGT365GDTY. Below, another offer a little bit more expensive, promo code: GITDFJISOPG25.

There are flexible tickets, exchangeable tickets, reimbursable tickets, and tickets that can't be exchanged. I'm a bit lost but it's important that I don't make a mistake. I'd like to be able to change train times at the last minute if I need to. Ah. More information about this ticket: click. "For more information about this type of ticket, please contact you travel agency."

Are they serious? I call the agency (they still exist but have one foot in the proverbial grave). "A ticket with the code GITDFJISOPG25? I don't know this code. I know HGSTSTVG41 or even TRAHKLST5K for this type of journey. But I mean, yeah. I can try and help you I guess." Yes! I've been trying to do this for 27 minutes. Help!

OK. In the end I finally understand what I need to do. I need to use the code GITDFJISOPG25. The other one is cheap, sure. But any kind of hitch, like a meeting running late or some traffic on the way to the station, and I'm screwed. Way too risky. And if for some reason I miss the train, it's me who has to pay. It would mean buying a very expensive ticket because it's last minute (and last minute tickets are very expensive indeed) and so it would be me who has the very expensive tab to pay as I should have anticipated this happening. So the Large Multinational Corporation's big idea to save money would end up costing a lot more, with a lot of validation emails and big bosses to back you up.

First step out of the way. But it's not over yet. Not at all. Now I need to find a budget code to complete the transaction. I click. A nice little window pops up. I marvel at the technology that has enabled me to see the 670 of budget codes for this category with only four buttons to navigate: Start/End and Previous/Next. Fortunately, there's a search function. One problem, the search doesn't work on the code part. No results. Great. I'm going to have to roll my sleeves up for this one. I don't have the choice. I'm going to have to go through 168 pages to find my code.

As you can imagine, sailing through this ocean of codes was a laugh a minute. The guys in finance really outdid themselves with this one in terms of pure creativity. After a few minutes sweating (what if I don't find it? What if I've already gone past it?), I see it. My wonderful little code, just for me, snuggled right in between 1954866321 and 1954866323. Lovely little code, I'm so happy that I found you. I'm so happy I feel positively joyful as I click you. Stay with me and never leave. I need you. I need you to go to London.

Code entered. Confirm, send. Soon, I'll be free.

"System error. Your code has not been recognized. Please contact the travel helpline."

The travel helpline. Quick. To the intranet. Ah, there's a special number. 602.

"Welcome to the interactive server. Please state the name of the person with whom you'd like to talk, or a key word." Yep, they even got rid of the lady who used to answer your calls. She even said "hello," and "how are you?" Too expensive obviously. Too expensive, takes up too much space and not fast enough. Not profitable and not efficient. Gone. Deleted.

Quickly, say the key word! "Travel". You have to say it clearly, proudly and while smiling. We're transferring you to the helpline." "Welcome to the Large Multinational Organization helpline." Some nice music. "Blah blah blah. If your call is concerning the Cats On Wheels incident, please press 1, otherwise please wait. Blah blah blah. More nice music.

"Hello. How can I help you?"

"Basically I've spent 53 minutes trying to book a trip for Paris/London on ZET. But it doesn't want to give me my budget code."

"OK ma'am, you're going to need to call the head of ZET or the helpline dedicated to travel."

So you have a couple of options at this point: kill yourself right there and then (no one will notice, there's no one left at the desks next to you, there are only robot voice servers left, the real humans are somewhere behind a desk, in front of a screen in a country much hotter than this one). Or just don't go to London.

Daily Report

2 large coffees, 1 expresso, 2 pieces of candy, 0 croissants.

My PC informs me that I have only 9 days left before I need to change my password to enter the network.

When I open a program, it informs me that I have only 8 days left before I need to change my password to enter the network.

Which one should I believe ?

Meeting Rooms

The human imagination, when put to use by a corporation (preferably Large and Multinational) reaches levels of development so high that it actually leaves the mortal realm and transcends to somewhere else entirely.

A random example. Meeting room names. In this bland, gray and austere world, let's add a little spice and exoticism. Let's voyage afar as we sleepwalk through these boring, repetitive meetings. Here's a few that I've seen over the 15 years of my professional life:

• The BIG European capitals: Rome, Berlin, London, Paris, Vienna, Madrid, Brussels, Stockholm.

• The BIG International cities: Melbourne, Mexico City, New York, Miami, Rio de Janeiro, Reykjavik, Bangkok.

• The BIG classical music composers: Chopin, Schubert, Mozart, Verdi, Bach, Schumann.

• The beautiful districts of Paris: Arc de Triomphe, Champs Elysées, Concorde, Opéra, Montmartre.

• Less poetic: 212A, 365B, Z785, P326, 001, 002, 003, 004, 85 East, 98 North, 2A6H34, 8B9S23.

But let's be honest, it would almost be impossible to organize a meeting at all if the rooms were named:

- After an African capital: Dakar, Nouakchott, Brazzaville, Kinshasa, Nairobi, Ouagadougou

- After a capital that's less "cool" (or that could put meeting participants in a combative mood): Bagdad, Kabul, Pyongyang, Grozny, Khartoum

- After a celebrity, rock group, pop star or rap artist: U2, Rolling Stones, Simple Minds, Kylie Minogue, Britney Spears, The Cure, Eminem, Pudgee the Fat Bastard

- A less glamourous town or city: Boring (Oregon, USA), Hell (Michigan, USA), Upton Snodsbury (Worcestershire, UK) Boogertown (North Carolina, USA), Barton in the Beans (Leicestershire, UK) or Humpybong (AUS).

Daily Report

Put my hands three times into the dusty, damp insides of the photocopier.

Twice turned out the lights in the toilet.

68 emails sent (I sent out a lot of invites), 6 received (3 spam and 2 personal).

1 conference call.

1 call with line busy.

The Christmas Tree

And all the while, Christmas has been approaching and has finally arrived. A little light that tries to shine among all of this nonsense. Guess what now lines each and every corridor of the Big Skyscraper? That's right, Christmas trees! Did you know: "Plants have a destressing effect on staff and induce an agreeable feeling of wellbeing, improves productivity and reduces absenteeism." That's what the guy selling the trees said, anyway.

In reality though, that is actually why we have the trees. To feel good despite the overwhelming sense of loneliness that takes over when we no longer understand just what really is going on and where we really are, and why we're here.

You'll never guess what they hung on the trees: a label shaped like a bauble, with "La Maison Tendresse " written on it.

Tenderness? The feeling of empathy and kindness? The altruistic life? Two pigeons in tender love? In this place? No comment.

WELCOME. THE ELEVATORS ARE TO THE RIGHT OF THE 3rd CHRISTMAS TREE!

Best Wishes - Part I

▶ □ ◀

Many strange and outdated traditions can be observed in the land of the Large Multinational Corporation during the season of goodwill. At our "House of Tenderness", it is still customary to spread the tender thoughts by sending our best wishes to people outside of the The Big Skyscraper.

Step 1: Discovering what the company Christmas card will look like. This year's design isn't exactly the most inspiring I've ever seen. Dull, insipid colors that depict a half-dead scene.

But this year we're lucky, because at least the card is easy to open. Yep. There have been a few years when even opening the card was a challenge. You fumbled around for a while trying to guess which side was the correct one, but to no avail. If, by a Christmas miracle, you somehow did manage to prize it open, you wouldn't even get so much as a funny little elf joyfully wishing you "Szzzzszzns Grrrrtngzzz!"

So this year they've decided that ease of opening is the Christmas card priority.

Step 2: Try to understand what is written inside. Every year, a thoughtful message is written on the card, and it's different each time. This year, they've decided to go for the theme "the world is complex." And they've really gone all out. We don't understand it, neither do you, and so now we're giving you a card that's also impossible to decipher. When you open the card, there are numbers and letters, but nothing makes any sense because the words are incomplete, in completely different fonts and sizes and all in different colors. It complicates the whole complexity of cracking the code to this cumbersome message.

The logo of the Large Multinational Corporation is somewhere in the middle of all this. Occasionally, it's used to replace a certain letter. Not always. This time, they just used it to make the card look prettier.

Step 3: To whom should I send this magnificent card?

Time to dust off the address book and dig out those business cards from the back of the drawer. I have a sudden moment of realization while doing this that arrives with such drama it must be linked to my general mood of the day. That is the realization that between the people I've lost contact with for reasons X or Y (usually Y), and those that I simply don't feel like sending my "Best Wishes" to (maybe I don't want to inflict this thing upon them; or on the other hand, perhaps such an ugly thing should only be sent to people we don't like), there are very few people indeed.

Wow, that's really not many people. Not many at all.

Well, everything's relative I suppose.

Anyway, I guess it will keep me busy for a little while. I'll add a little message of my own, sign my name, slip a little business card into the envelope (so they're sure who it's from), and fling that thing into the outbox.

Daily Report

32 ugly Christmas cards sent.

80 useless and uninteresting contacts in my address book.

Best Wishes – Part II

▶□◀

The first day back at work after the holidays is when the "greetings" fun really steps up another notch entirely. No matter what you're doing or where you are, for the entire month of January, as soon as you see someone else in the corridor, elevator, in front of their desk, in the restrooms, the food court, a meeting room, by email, telephone or chat... you know what you need say, each and every time?

Happy New Year!

I always wonder what the best way to do this is.

• Perhaps we should note down the names of all those we've said it to and those we haven't yet, so that:

a. You don't say it twice to the same person (It's important not to waste time, except then you don't get to say "Oh well, better to say it twice than not at all, amirite ?" That would be a real shame. Or not really, in fact. Not at all suits me just fine.)

b. You can check regularly to whom you have yet to say it, and so plan surreptitious meetings with a few of them while carefully continuing to avoid others.

• Can we change what we say?

a. Have an awesome new year! (quite informal)

b. Have a lovely new year! (a bit too... informal)

c. Have an excellent new year, full of happiness, good health and professional success for you and your loved ones (a bit too long)

d. Yo! This year is gonna be freakin' amazing! (a bit to young)

e. Mmm hmm! It's going to be a sweet and beautiful new year! (a bit flirtatious)

f. Have a totally killer new year bro! (way too young and informal)

- Should we do something else while saying it?

a. Shaking hands (too masculine)

b. With a warm hug (look at how much we love each other)

c. With a big slap on the back (WAY too masculine)

d. With a wet kiss on the cheek (more feminine. At least one person should be a girl)

e. With a few wet kisses (you might be very popular for the day)

f. By stepping on their toes (reserved for enemies only)

g. By stepping on both of their feet (reserved for your very worst enemies!)

h. With an apologetic smile (I like you really)

i. With a monstrous frown (Best not!)

Are you allowed to say it in more interesting ways? Can you rap it, for example? Can you be a little inappropriate, or subversive, perhaps ?

HA! Imagine the anarchy that would bring to the Large Multinational Corporation.

Still, there are only 29 days left to go until the end of January. Have to keep it together.

Daily Report

Turned off the restroom lights twice (I'm going to stop going there).

1 coffee, 54 text messages, 321 emails.

Best Wishes – Part III

▶□◀

Since the arrival of email, this incredible new technology has transformed the way we communicate.

Now, thanks to email, you can send nice little messages to your colleagues, your team, your professional network, and basically anyone else who has even the vaguest link to the multidimensional matrix of the Large Multinational Corporation. Especially when it's the new year. Everyone gets involved by sending their very own sterile little messages.

Like the boss sending one to his obedient little slaves:

"20XX was a tough year, but we got through it (more like survived it. Well, the ones who are still here). 20XX+1we will be even better, you'll see. It will be a great year for us. Big things are going to happen. And as long as there's hope, there's life. Feel free to pass this message on to those who are close to you: family, friends, etc. etc."

Stay strong boys and girls. We're almost good. Regarding the part about your family and friends, it's to remind you that you have them. Remember? Those people you don't see any more because of meetings that run late or a business trip on the other side of the planet? The people that you live (lived?) with when you are not spending your nights at the Large

Multinational Corporation. How big it is of them to remind us.

Or a message from the Project Manager to their sweating workers:

"It's wonderful to work with you. Next year will be even better. Be happy with yourselves. Every day I get happier and happier to be working with you on the Cats project."

Liars, all of them. Fake messages of love circulating the fake House of Tenderness. Personally, I don't give two hoots about the message sent by the co-manager on the 35th floor, who has spent the entire year trying to catch me out, throwing banana skins left, right and center so I mess up the Thingummy file.

The basic message is no longer been enough though. For the past two or three years, it's been considered necessary (cool) to add a little GIF, too. A little flashing Christmas tree, a swinging bauble, some holly that shivers, a sparkling wreath, a rabbit that appears out of a hat, a bell that moves back and forth, a melting snowman, and many more besides. Something that gives it a personal touch, that when couple with text, gives it some color, a little movement. It makes you look nicer in the eyes of the recipients.

And I, well I think about all those Christmas trees, baubles, the holly, wreaths, rabbits, bells and snowmen who brighten things up with their flashing, shivering, sparkling, swinging, trapped as a string of zeros and ones, 01111000011100100101, on a server somewhere on the other side of the world. It's all good! But oh, how they must be laughing, as they peer out at us from behind our screens, as they try in vain to add a little sparkle to our lives.

Daily Report

41 ridiculous "Season's Greetings" emails received.

0 "Season's Greetings" emails sent (I'm on strike).

Epilogue

What if I've seen enough of this now?

What if I updated my CV this year?

It's a good time to turn my wavering attention toward the uninviting world of global recruitment but also to continue having fun with global work in a smaller enterprise in the 3.0 era.

Acknowledgements

▶□◀

I would like to extend my sincere thanks to:

All those with whom I met eyes that inspired me without knowing it,

All of the blog readers and those who read extracts from this book who gave me positive feedback and whom I made laugh,

All of the blog readers who gave me negative feedback, in doing so letting me know that I left no one indifferent,

Renard, who has given me the most incredible support by giving me his time and his talent in illustrating my prose,

My husband, assiduous proofreader, for his encouragement and continuous support,

My children, for their enthusiasm for life which helps me to move forward,

Folco Chevallier, for his coaching and support through the BookLeaders program,

All of the businessmen and still-too-rare businesswomen who I met in various airports around this beautiful planet of ours,

All of the overheated servers around the world (who still overheat despite all the air conditioning),

And to you, the person who has just read this book, and whom I hope will take the time to leave a little review on Amazon or my Facebook page: www.facebook.com/GlobalWorkCollection/.

Thalia NeoMedia / DG Editions Les Funambulles

First printed: October 2019

ISBN : 978-2-491222-00-0